THE VICTORIAN
CHAISE LONGUE

MARGHANITA LASKI

The Victorian Chaise Longue

Academy
Chicago
Publishers

© Copyright 1953 by Marghanita Laski
Published in 1984 by

Academy Chicago, Publishers
425 N. Michigan Avenue
Chicago, Illinois 60611

Printed and bound in the U.S.A.

Library of Congress Cataloging in Publication Data

Laski, Marghanita, 1915–
    The Victorian chaise longue.

    I.   Title.
PR6023.A72V5   1984   823'.914   84-425
ISBN 0-89733-097-8 (pbk.)

TO JOHN HAYWARD

I am dying in my own death and
the deaths of those after me.

T. S. Eliot

****
*   *
*   *
*   *
*   *
*   *
*   *1*   *
*   *
*   *
*   *
*   *
*   *
*   *
****

"WILL YOU GIVE ME YOUR WORD OF honour," said Melanie, "that I am not going to die?"

The doctor said, "It's a stupid thing to ask of me. Of course you're going to die, and so am I, and so is Guy, and in the end even Richard is going to die. What you're really asking me is whether you're going to die soon of tuberculosis, and to that the answer is no, though I'm not giving any word of honour about it."

Melanie reared up from the nest of pillows. "Why not?" she demanded. "Why won't you, if you're really sure?"

The doctor said sternly, "Lie down." He waited until she had obediently let herself sink back into the big square pillows, their pink linen cases faintly shining with the glaze the good laundries still gave the good linen, lending their pale pink glow to the pretty little pale face with its fuzz of child-soft yellow hair. "Jumping about like that," he said with mock reproof. "Do you wonder I won't give any promises?"

But Melanie felt safer now, she in her nest and he with a smile on his face. She smiled back, meaning to say only that she loved and trusted him, and the doctor wondered again how it was that Melanie's smile seemed always to invite delights he was sure she had never known. "It's a long time since I've seen you smile like that," he said; yes, it was a long time, now that he came to think of it, not since — "It's all right to smile now," said Melanie, "now that I know I'm not going to die," but she could not help her voice rising in interrogation as she ended.

The doctor sighed. "If I'd known how obstreperous one negative reaction would have made you," he said, "I'd never have told you about it." He twitched his chair closer to her bed and for the hundredth time misjudged its weight and wondered irritably why Guy had never told Melanie that papier-mâché chairs with fancy inlays might look very pretty in a lady's bedroom, but that gentlemen visitors wanted something a bit more substantial to sit on. "Now listen to me," he said. "Because you've managed to be a good obedient girl so far, we've been able to conquer what might have been a very nasty little flare-up, and if you let yourself get perfectly well and we keep a steady eye on you, there's no reason why anything of the sort should ever occur again."

"Not even if I have another baby?" asked Melanie.

"Well, I wouldn't have *too* many," said the doctor cautiously, "but the trouble was lying in wait before you started Richard, you know. I doubt whether it would have become active so quickly if you hadn't been pregnant, but, of course, it might have flared up at any time."

"It was lucky it waited so long, though, wasn't it?" said Melanie, smiling again.

"Very lucky," said the doctor grimly. Melanie should never fully understand how lucky it was that after they'd decided to take the chance of letting the pregnancy continue, the suspicious patch had become active only after the baby had become viable, so that the urgently performed induction could give her a healthy son. "But that was only — let me see — only seven months ago," he said, continuing his train of thought rather than the conversation. "There's not got to be any high jinks, not for a long time yet. We'll spend the summer just as peacefully and quietly as we can, and soon as the weather starts to get nasty, off you go to Switzerland, with that husband of yours to keep a firm eye on you."

"And Richard," said Melanie, still unable to be sure that what was left unsaid need not be feared or distrusted.

"And Richard," the doctor agreed. "Nanny looking forward to going among foreigners?"

"Sister says she is," said Melanie. She was beginning to sparkle. Soon, the doctor knew, she would become excited and giggling and vivacious, and soon after the still scanty store of health would be burnt up, and tomorrow Melanie would be lying back exhausted, pleading feverishly again that he would promise that she wasn't going to die. "But in the meantime," he said with emphasis, "we've got to go on exactly as we've been doing, no frolics, no excitement, the very utmost care and circumspection. You've got to treat yourself as if — " his eyes roamed round the pretty bedroom, over the creamy silky paper on the walls, the shiny cream curtains printed with huge pink roses, the rosewood bedhead decked with cavorting French brasses, and then to the mirror on the lace-frilled dressing table, rosy-flushed cherubs clambering in and out of wreaths of coloured posies, and there he found his analogy and ended, " — as if you were a piece of Dresden china."

"Who's a piece of Dresden china?" asked Guy, coming in, carrying two glasses of sherry. "Is my Melly a piece of Dresden china, then?" he asked playfully, handing one glass to the doctor and then sitting on the bed, not forgetting first to set his own glass on the bedside table in order to hitch up the soberly striped trousers, insignia of the rising young barrister, the clubbable likeable rising young man. Why don't I really like him? the doctor asked himself again, I never really expected — after all, I've known Melanie almost since she was a child — and once again he thrust the obtrusive thought away, telling himself fiercely that he'd no patience with a lot of that psychiatrical nonsense, anyone would be jealous of a young

6

man so well endowed, so confidently expectant, that he could afford to leave a practice barely established in order to accompany his wife to Switzerland for six months. And a good thing too, he decided unkindly; for all Master Guy's pretty ways with her, he doesn't look like a man who's been deprived of what he fancies these last months. "I was telling Melanie that that's the way she's got to look after herself," he said shortly.

"And so she shall," Guy reassured him. "Shan't you, my pretty love?" He began to play with her fingers, and his voice took on the mock — and yet not so mock — pomposity of his humour as he continued, "The use of the phrase Dresden china as a synonym for expensive fragility suggests that there were lamentable gaps in Britain's nineteenth-century supremacy over world markets. And how strange that it should be the Germans, themselves almost synonymous with heaviness, clumsiness, everything that is the antithesis of the object of which we speak, who have provided the very phrase that leaps into your mind when you feel the need to warn Melanie that she must be the object of our incessant, our unremitting care — " it needed a new breath, after all, to complete the sentence; Guy took it as unobtrusively as possible, and ended triumphantly, " — as of her own."

"How clever you are, darling," said Melanie adoringly. "You make me feel so silly compared with you."

"But I like you silly," said Guy, and so he does, thought Dr. Gregory, watching them. But Melanie isn't the fool he thinks her, not by a long chalk; she's simply the purely feminine creature who makes herself into anything her man wants her to be. Not that I'd call her clever, rather cunning — his thoughts checked, a little shocked at the word he had chosen, but he continued resolutely — yes, cunning as a cartload of monkeys if ever she needed to be. But she won't, he told himself, and wondered why he felt so relieved to know that Melanie was loved and protected and, in so far as anything could possibly be sure, safe.

Now he watched her pouting and saying to Guy in pretended distress, "Dr. Gregory won't promise me that I'm not going to die," and husband and wife, their hands still clasped, looked almost furtively towards the doctor, not daring to let their faces betray either amusement or apprehension.

The doctor pushed back his chair and stood up. "You're trying to force my hand, young woman," he said, "and I'm not going to let you get away with it. This is the very last time I'm going to make my little speech. Fourteen months ago, seven months before young Richard was born, Dr. Macpherson and I discovered a suspicious patch on that left lung of yours, and both of us suggested that it wouldn't be a bad idea to count this particular baby out, and start in with a new one when we'd got everything cleared up. But rightly, as it turned out — or as I hope it's going to turn out — we agreed to let you keep your baby on the clear understanding that if things got any worse, there wouldn't be any baby till next time and that next time might be a good deal further away as a result. When we said this, we both hoped, as you know, that the suspicious patch would remain just that, but it turned nasty, as these things are apt to do, and though, by the greatest good fortune, we've presented you with a fine bouncing baby, you've got to remember for a long time yet that you've had a lot of active tuberculous bacilli floating around in you as well."

But Melanie had stopped listening. She liked the speech to be made, liked its solemnity that centred so decisively in herself, but after the happy ending, she never listened to the warning. "Dr. Gregory talks as if it was he who made the baby," she said to Guy, "but it wasn't, it was us, wasn't it?"

"Alone we did it," agreed Guy, but added courteously to the doctor, "though I will admit that we had some very necessary help in the process. I went up to see him now," he said to Melanie. "He was lying on his tummy having his bottom wiped, and sucking his thumb furiously."

"Oh the darling!" cried Melanie. Her eyes swept from her husband to the doctor, and she demanded, "When am I going to see him properly, not just held up at the door, here, here, here?" She thumped the bed beside her where the baby should lie and had never lain.

The doctor sighed, knowing that his warnings had been useless, wondering whether he should again remind her that every kind of excitement and intensity must be resolutely avoided — but excitement and intensity, he had always known, were Melanie's response to life. For eight months she had obediently lain still in bed, but with the stillness of taut anger and resentment and never the demanded relaxation. Her large blue eyes had spoken passionately of misery and impatience and yearning with little need for the voice she had been bidden to use so sparingly, to speak only of essential needs and never waste her breath on complaint or love. Each day as he came into the room, the doctor had looked to see if Melanie's eyes were yet resigned, but now he knew that they would never be, that they always would be resentful and angry until he could once again allow them to be gay.

You had to reckon, said the doctor to himself, that with Melanie as much energy went into lying still as most women spent in a day at the sales. He repeated the warning again. "You've only had one negative reaction, you know, only one, and already you're behaving as if you could climb the Matterhorn."

"I'm sorry," said Melanie imploringly, "but it was the test that did it, you know. I've been going on and on being good, and then suddenly knowing that the test was all right made it seem as if we'd got somewhere at last, and I feel I just can't go on. Something new and exciting has simply got to happen."

I'd better tell her, the doctor decided. He said, "Well, we are going to let something happen, something very exciting indeed. I told Dr. Macpherson the result of our last test when I saw him at the hospital this morning, just before I came along here, and we agreed that if you produce three good results, all in a row, we'll let you have Richard to play with."

As he had expected, by the time he had finished Melanie was sitting bolt upright in bed, suffused with excitement. He sighed theatrically and instantly she shot down again. Why, in heaven's name, can't she do things gently, said the doctor to himself.

Even now, though she lay obediently back, her grip on Guy's hand had tightened to expose the tense muscle running up her arm. "Do you hear that, darling, do you hear?" she cried to Guy. "He's going to give me my baby — oh, Guy, do you think he'll know me, won't it be awful if he doesn't like me, do you think it's too late — "

She'll be in tears in a minute unless there's some diversion, thought the doctor grimly. He said, "And now you've got something ahead of you to keep you quiet, what do you say to a little treat to be going on with? — if you can keep quiet for just a minute and let me tell you about it."

"Of course I can keep quiet — I am quiet," said

Melanie reproachfully, lifting big imploring eyes to his, and he said, "What do you say to a little change of view? Not that it isn't very pretty looking out of this window, with all these acacias, but you've probably had more than enough of them for a bit, and a change is good for everyone."

"Do you mean," cried Melanie, "that I'm going to be able to get out of this room?"

The doctor nodded.

When they had first decided to buy the house, enjoying the shocked incredulity of both sets of parents who had insisted that no one could live there, back of the railways, down by the canal, why, it was no better than a slum, then Melanie would never have thought it possible that the pretty bedroom she planned would one day seem like a prison. How much she and Guy had enjoyed the informed superiority with which they had worsted the protesting parents, able to point out that already an artist and an architect had bought and reclaimed homes in this hidden forgotten Regency row ("Artists and architects aren't barristers," his father had said. "That sort of gentry don't look at things like we do."), and later two more homes had been reclaimed and converted, one by a young professor and the other by a senior Civil Servant whose name even the parents knew, leaving only one house still held firmly in working-class hands, the object of complicated plots hatched by the other owners on summer evenings when they brought their glasses of sherry out into the little front gardens behind the paved rope-walk that bordered the canal. And how much the houses had changed since the Langdons had first come there, two years ago. Then they had all looked alike, dirty brick and dirty paint and dirty lace curtains, and only the gardens were different, here a rockery and here a gnome and there some green-and-white minia-ture palings. Now the gardens were identical, each neatly paved with thick rectangular stones, and, set in each, spindly white-painted iron chairs and table, and it was the houses that had grown apart from their neighbours and changed, what with the grey front door and the turquoise, the shiny black and the con-sciously amusing light fumed oak, the studio on top of the artist's house, and on Guy's and Melanie's the new top storey, a present from his parents, to house the coming baby with night nursery, day nursery and bathroom.

"But of course you must choose the colours," Sister Smith had said, coaxing and encouraging, when Melanie would push away the swatches and the sam-ples, saying that it didn't matter anyway, because the baby wouldn't live and neither would she. But Sister had been right to insist so patiently that it should be Melanie who decided, for it meant that when she sent her thoughts exploring round the house, she knew that the day nursery was white and scarlet and the night nursery yellow and blue; but though Sister had tried to keep her amused by drawing little plans, she could never perfectly visualise the rooms and be sure how the nursing chair looked in three dimensions but saw it always as a rectangular patch on a piece of paper with "nursing chair" in Sister's writing inside it, and the only three-dimensional reality left was the bedroom from which all flavour of love and joy and delight had long since fled.

"I think we'll have Sister in on this," said Dr. Gregory, getting up from his chair and opening the door that led through into the drawing room, and there, patiently waiting, was Sister — Melanie could see her from the bed — standing by the window, turning over the new Vogue, always leaving the bedroom as soon as the strictly professional part of the consultation was over, but always waiting in the drawing room in case she was wanted, not climbing to the blue-and-yellow night nursery where she slept, Nanny having willingly agreed that for the moment, and seeing how things were, she and Baby could make out nicely with just the front room.

"I've been telling Mrs. Langdon that we think she deserves a change of view," said the doctor playfully, and Sister matched his geniality in her rich Irish voice. "I'm thinking she won't be saying no to *that*," she said, and they both gazed benevolently on Melanie, the good child promised the treat.

"Now let's see," said Dr. Gregory, using his working voice once more as he made a professional evaluation of the situation. "You're facing east in here, aren't you, so you're already getting all the morning sun that's going. But if we let you move into the drawing room in the afternoons, we could toast you properly, as soon as this blessed summer decides to get going."

"There won't be much point in moving if it just goes on raining," said Melanie, discovering that a change, after so long, was alarming.

"Now, it's always you lucky people who grumble," said Sister, not quite lightly enough. "Why, I shouldn't be a bit surprised if even the sun himself didn't make a special effort to shine for you."

"The practical question to be considered," Dr. Gregory said, "is what we've got in the drawing room we can make you comfortable on." He opened the communicating door again, and Guy rose from beside Melanie's bed and came to look over his shoulder.

At first sight it didn't seem very promising. Facing the fireplace there stood a little painted Empire settee that Guy and Melanie had always themselves refrained from sitting on, though guests had never positively complained, and no one could deny that it was extremely pleasant to look at and perfect with the elegant gold urns on the mock-Empire wallpaper. There were two comfortable modern armchairs and a stiff little armless padded chair on which Melanie had imagined herself sitting and knitting during the last months of her pregnancy, the golden head bent over the white wool and the withdrawn heaven-touched face compensating for the misshapen body. But before the knitting wool had even been bought, Melanie had been confined, helpless and raging, to her bed, and beside her the knitting had been done, swiftly and beautifully but surely not with the love, by Sister Smith. Melanie's memories followed the doctor's exploratory glance round the drawing room, and as he turned to Guy to say, "I don't quite see —" Melanie eagerly interrupted with, "I could lie on the Victorian chaise longue."

"The how-much?" exclaimed the doctor, turning round quickly, and Guy said, "Yes, she's perfectly right. Look!" and, taking the doctor's arm, he pulled him round the door to the wall that the door's opening had masked. And there stood the Victorian chaise longue.

It was ugly and clumsy and extraordinary, nearly seven feet long and proportionately wide. The head and foot ends of the seat curled round a little as though to meet each other, raising, above the elaborately carved legs and frame, a superstructure of wine-red crimson felt. At the right-hand end a curved padded support rolled backwards on curlicues of carving and a carved framework supported padding to halfway down the back. Its Regency ancestor had probably been delicate and enchanting; this descendant was gross, and would certainly have been inadmissible in such a home as Guy's and Melanie's were it not for the singular startling quality of the berlin-wool cross-stitch embroidery that sprawled in bright gigantic roses over the shabby felt, over the curved half-back and right from the top of the headrest to the very end of the seat.

"What a monstrous thing!" said the doctor. "Wherever did you find it?" and, not waiting for an answer, he added, "I should think it would do very well."

Melanie had found the Victorian chaise longue on her last day of freedom when the threatening cloud was no larger than a man's hand and could still, as by the finding of the chaise longue, be replaced in her vision by toys.

"But I think we'll have the next examination in my consulting room," Dr. Gregory had said, when she had called him in to confirm the superb news of pregnancy. "We'll want a really thorough checkup, you know," and so the day before finding the chaise longue she had obediently called on Dr. Gregory in his tall thin house behind the Marylebone Road. "You can get your clothes on now," he had said, and disappeared, and when she came from behind the screen, he had looked up from his notes with an odd expression on his face and said, "I think I'd like you to see a specialist."

Melanie had laughed at his surprisingly worried expression, and laughing brought on, as it so often did, the painful little cough she'd thought was from too much smoking. Gasping for breath between laughing and coughing, she had managed to get out, "Well, don't look so upset about it — you fix it when it suits you," and the fear had begun when Dr. Gregory grimly answered, "I'll fix it for tomorrow."

He had gone out of the room, and she heard the bell as he lifted the telephone receiver, but what he said was muffled by the door and the heavy curtain that hung over it. She sat down by the desk, frowning slightly and wondering why she felt uneasy, because hadn't everyone always said that that was the splendid thing about Dr. Gregory, he never took any chances, but whipped you off to a specialist as soon as he had the slightest doubt. Then he came back into the room and said curtly, "Dr. Macpherson's secretary has managed to fit you in at quarter past twelve tomorrow. Here's the address. I'll meet you there."

She had taken the slip of paper he held out to her, still uneasily puzzled, and it was to try to drive away her own uncertainty that she had stated with just a faint note of questioning, "I suppose this Dr. Macpherson is a gynaecologist?" and in the pause before Dr. Gregory's answer, the fear was not dispelled but confirmed.

Dr. Gregory had put a finger on the little letter scales that stood on his desk, held the bascule down and released it to a small brassy clang. Looking not at Melanie but at the machine, he had said, with too careful nonchalance, "Well, no, he's not actually a gynaecologist. As a matter of fact he's *the* man on chests — you must have heard of him, Horace Macpherson — and I just want him to take a quick look at yours. There's nothing like taking all precautions in good time, you know," and then he had looked up at her and smiled, willing her to accept the reassurance.

But there had been too much uneasiness in the air for that. "He thinks I've got T.B.," Melanie had wept to Guy as soon as he got home that evening, imploring him to deny it with sufficient vehemence to make it untrue, but all the denials he could make went no further than words, and soon it was *his* doubt and fear that Melanie must in her turn try to allay.

"But it's absolute nonsense," he would say, "you know that really, darling, don't you? — though, mind you, he's perfectly right to take every possible precaution." And Melanie, "Why, of course it isn't anything, darling, I'm sure it's a good idea to be absolutely sure, and we'll be laughing at this tomorrow, it's only that tonight . . . " She lay in his arms between the pink linen sheets, whispering. "I know I'm being silly, darling, I know I'm being silly, but I'm so frightened" — until very late, long after midnight, he had made love to her from a desperate need to feel her alive around him, their two bodies linked in the epitome of life. But it was no use. The failure of her response seemed a symbolic failure, and afterwards she had wept that she was sorry, that she knew she wasn't any good, but she couldn't stop thinking, thinking about tomorrow. This was the last time they had lain in each other's arms and made love.

But it was of love that Melanie had thought when she first saw the Victorian chaise longue. She had left the house much too early for the appointment, for, this morning, the hitherto delightful routine had been impossible. "Order what you like, Trude," she said, with no heart for the long discussion, the telephone orders to the amiable shopkeepers, the pleasant consciousness of performing traditional duties. "Say I've gone out," she called when the telephone rang. Usually when her tasks were done, she would sit in the window seat in the drawing room and look down at the dark shiny canal, all her mind on great and little delights, but this day she had not gone into the drawing room, only taken the car and driven off, down the wide derelict streets at the back of the little house, through the thronging commercial traffic by the stations, along Euston Road until she got to Harley Street — and there she was, much too early, and so she started the car again and drove slowly in and out of the lanes that lie between Harley Street and Baker Street, turning, signalling, changing gear, driving on and on because it was something to do that was more than waiting and being afraid, until, in a very small street behind Marylebone Lane, she came to an antique shop neither she nor Guy had yet discovered.

Antique shops, or junk shops, as they called them, were their common hobby. On Saturday mornings, dressed, so they believed, like people who haggled not from pleasure but because they must, they would leave the car well away out of sight, and wander up and down the Chalk Farm Road, the Portobello Road, St. Christopher's Place, looking for the pretty sparkles that would embellish and cement the nest. "We really do need some Bristol glass for the dining room," one or the other would say, "A Victorian china bell for the bedroom, a bamboo canterbury," and the need was real enough, even if its immediate focus no more than a random justification. So, "I really do need a cradle," Melanie said to herself when she saw the hitherto undiscovered shop, and she remembered the cradle of Napoleon's baby son, the King of Rome, that she had read of as a child, a cradle shaped like a boat with a gilded prow, and she imagined such a cradle standing on the needlework flowers of the rug before the drawing-room fire, rocked by her pretty foot to content the plump drowsy baby who sucked his thumb oblivious of the decorous sherry-drinking above his head. "May I just look round?" she asked the elegant young man (new pattern of shopkeepers, the narrow trousers, the velvet smoking jacket), obedient to the belief that if you asked for the object immediately, your bargaining position was irrevocably ruined. So she examined a bead footstool with feigned absorption, asked the price of a sepia

Bartolozzi printed on rotting ivory satin, and then, putting this down with pretended regret, she asked casually, as if by way of after-thought, whether by any odd chance they'd got a cradle.

As a matter of fact they had, answered the young man, but it was in the basement, would she mind coming down, look out for the stairs, sorry about the dust. It's a miracle, thought Melanie, as she always did when they had what she asked for, somewhere tucked away, and groping down the stone steps she forgot, for the first time, the appointment waiting at quarter past twelve.

But, as so often, the miracle failed, and just as the promised Bristol glass would turn out to be bright blue china and the Victorian china bell unmistakably Edwardian, so the cradle was Jacobean, dark carved oak and hopelessly unfashionable. "I can't say I fancy it myself," admitted the young man. "It will probably go to America. There's quite a demand for them there, for keeping logs in, you know."

"*My* cradle will have a baby in it," said Melanie proudly, and they enjoyed a moment of sympathetic superiority, the poor yet well-adjusted English who hadn't lost sight of true purposes.

The Victorian chaise longue had been stacked upside down on top of a pile of furniture, its clumsy legs threshing the air like an unclipped sheep that had tumbled on to its back, its rich wine-red wool-embroidered underside spread like a canopy over the marble-topped washstand on top of the round mahogany table. "That looks rather exciting," Melanie had said, adding cautiously, "Goodness knows what one would do with it."

"It's not in very good condition, I'm afraid," said the young man. "There isn't much demand for these late ones. I've got a little Regency day bed you might like, if that's the kind of thing you're after."

"It's this one that's taken my fancy," said Melanie, suddenly forgetting the need for feigned disinterest, and speaking from a profound want of this Victorian sofa.

"Well, we'll get it down for you to have a proper look at it," said the young man, and Hal was called from the workroom at the back, and the chaise longue was shifted and upended, and at last set right side up on the dusty flagstone floor.

"It seems to have got a bit stained," said the young man, as they stood side by side, looking down on it. He pointed to a brownish stain on the seat, discolouring a pale pink rose and the dark red felt underneath it, as if something had been carelessly spilt there.

"It hardly shows," said Melanie, as if she were the salesman now. "Have you got room for it?" he asked, he too accepting this reversal of the roles, and discarding his proper duty of titillating and praising for the customer's part of hesitant withdrawal. "I'll make room," said Melanie. "I shall lie on it after my baby's born," not noticing that this was the first time she had indicated her pregnancy to a stranger. From long-enjoyed usage of daydreams, she tried to envisage the frail young mother in the floating clouds of negligée, the tender faces of solicitous admiring friends, but the picture remained in unfelt words, and instead of it there was only her body's need to lie on the Victorian chaise longue, that, and an overwhelming assurance, or was it a memory, of another body that painfully crushed hers into the berlin-wool?

But she had never lain on the chaise longue yet. The young man hadn't asked a high price, nor had she tried to beat him down. For a ridiculously small sum she had bought the chaise longue and left the shop and gone to keep her appointment in Harley Street; but by the time the chaise longue had been delivered to the house by the canal, Melanie's body was confined alone in the bedroom behind the drawing room, and all her waking moments she was hopelessly crying.

"Is it comfortable enough?" Dr. Gregory asked now, and through the double doors Melanie heard him smacking it smartly. "It's not bad at all," he said with surprise. "Horsehair, it must be; there's a lot to be said for these old horsehair fillings," and, coming back into the bedroom, "Well, Melanie, do you fancy an afternoon on those hideous roses?"

So they fixed her up there after lunch, telling Trude, first, to give the sofa a good brush-down and to light a fire in the polished steel grate. Guy pushed away the little Empire settee and with some difficulty pulled the chaise longue into its place, with its head facing the delicate long windows, and then Sister, after a consultation at the linen cupboard with Nanny, brought down an armful of pink blankets, and arranged them into a soft warm nest.

"Now for the great moment," said Guy, and he lifted Melanie out of bed, swiftly through the double doors and onto the chaise longue, Sister hovering beside him, ready instantly to tuck the blankets in tightly round Melanie's thin body.

They both stood beside the chaise longue, looking down on her in triumph, for here at last was the proof to confirm the hopeful words that had been so often repeated for so many months — "No, you won't die . . ." "Yes, you are getting better . . ." "Yes, really, truly, I promise, I swear . . ." "I'm nearly better," Melanie said with delight, and Guy took her hand and held it to his lips. "You're very nearly perfectly well," he said, and in a glow, "Darling, isn't it wonderful!" while Sister smiled proudly, the satisfied craftsman.

"I must get back," said Guy. "I've got some people coming to chambers at three." "The best thing Mrs. Langdon can do now," said Sister, "is to take her nap, after all this excitement." "I'll get back for tea if I possibly can," Guy promised, and Sister said, "Now that's a very good idea. You can both take your tea together in your drawing room to-day like Christian people, and if that isn't a real treat, I don't know what is. Would you like me to draw the curtains, Mrs. Langdon?" she asked, but Melanie said no, the view and the sunlight would help her to go to sleep.

"Then I'll leave it to Mr. Langdon to shut you up," said Sister, and rustled away into the bedroom, closing the double doors behind her.

"Darling!" said Melanie to Guy, holding up her arms to him, and he came close to her and clasped her to him, their first embrace for so very long that held the certain promise of continued happiness.

Through the open windows the spring poured in. From her couch, bathed in the soft sweet air, Melanie could not see the canal that lay beside her home, but it flowed through her imagination, dark and still and beautiful. From the water on the far side, a rough bank rose steeply to a bombed, still desolate waste, and from one of the brambles that sprawled all over it, a branch curved high and free to lie across the blue sky in the window, dark leaves and paper-pink flowers suffused with sunlight faintly swaying across the pale blue sky. Drowsy, Melanie looked at the flowers and the sky, and the noises of the city — the soft continuous roar of traffic, the whine of the milkman's electric cart that stopped and started in the street behind — died away with her slow beatific loss of immediacy. A child called to another in the gardens along the terrace, and then these clear incoherent voices faded and were lost. Nearly asleep, nearly asleep — and the oboe began to play — that's Elizabeth next door, thought Melanie in pleased recognition, her last conscious thought before the mental formlessness of slumber. And as she lay there, so nearly, so very nearly asleep, she was unthinkingly aware of the sky and the flowers and the music, of the sun-warmed air on her body that was at last sure of happiness to come. Time died away, the solitary burden of human life was transformed in glory, and Melanie, withdrawn in ecstasy, fell asleep.

2

SHE OPENED HER EYES AND IT WAS DARK. I am still asleep, she thought, and she shut her eyes again; but soon she realised that it was not now the delightful chaos of sleep still imposed on her brain. Now, this time, I am really awake, she said, and again she opened her eyes and again it was dark, darkness charged with a faint foul smell.

She moved her hand a little, brushing it over what covered her breast, and it was not the touch of soft pink wool but harsh rough strangeness. The touch and the smell and the darkness, all were strange. It could have been any conceivable period of time in which the thought that all these were strange took shape and words.

She opened her mouth and there came, not the shriek that deafened her brain, but a strangled mew, dispersed as soon as sounded, leaving no awareness, and still the time passing was unaccountable. Then a sound, a door opening (but it took a long time to translate the noise into comprehension), and a woman said, "Well, Milly? Are you ready to wake up now?"

A common voice, a cruel voice, assured and domineering. Not a voice to be conquered with superior strength but the nightmare voice that binds the limbs in dreadful paralysis while the danger creeps and creeps and at last will leap. I am asleep, said Melanie, ordering her wakened brain to admit this and be still, her closed eyes to see not even the ugly green and scarlet and yellow patterns under too tightly pressed eyelids, and then there was a heavy weighted rattle and almost simultaneously another, and consciousness of light shot through the closed lids and forced them open.

She was looking towards the rattling noise, up and away to the right at a window, first, draped heavily patterned lace curtains against a leaden grey sky, then — the vision widening without wish, without will — the thick mahogany bar across the top of the window, the thick brass rings still quivering a little, below them the dark red-brown plush curtains still shaking, and, her hand still on the fringed loop that held the dark curtains away from the lace, a woman.

"Who are you?" whispered Melanie, and then quicker and quicker, "Who are you, who are you?"

"That's enough of that," said the woman. "Wake up properly, now, and no more of your nonsense." She slipped the brass ring of the fringed loop over its brass hook in the window frame, then gave the folds of the curtains a twitch that brought them into symmetry with those on the other side. "Still that nasty fog," the *a* short and open.

Melanie said with careful articulation, "I am asleep. Will you please go away so that I can shut my eyes and wake up." She did not close her mouth when she had finished; it hung flaccidly open as she herself hung in this no-time of the dream.

The woman shrugged her shoulders, and for the first time Melanie translated observation into mental words. She had very sloping shoulders, she said silently, but she did not examine the meaning of the thought, only tried to stifle it because it had come in words, and once thoughts came in words, the conscious mind chose to use more and more of them until it was impossible to go to sleep again and only waking was left. "But it's waking-up I want to do," she said aloud in bewilderment, and the woman said roughly, "Pull yourself together, Milly. A girl can wake up without all this to-do," though it wasn't "girl" she said, but something nearer "gal," and as she spoke, she came away from the window and stood at Melanie's feet, between Melanie and the fireplace.

"Why do you wear those clothes?" asked Melanie. Every word she had spoken since she first opened her eyes came out of her mouth without thought or will, and it was only now, having asked the question, that

33

she looked at the woman, looked, that is to say, with her brain behind her eyes, forming into coherent thought all that her eyes perceived.

The clothes of which Melanie had spoken went down to the ground. The clothes were a black dress high to the neck, smoothly projecting out then curving in over a strangely shaped bosom, falling thickly from the waist to the ground. The sleeves were long, widening below the elbow, and from beneath them white frills of heavy lace were caught in at the wrists to leave no flesh visible between them and the black mittens encasing the hands. The shoulders sloped upwards to the high neck, edged by a narrow white frill, and in the centre of its fastening was a big oval brooch, a streaked glossy red-brown stone in a frame of twisted gold.

"Give over your silly questions, do," said the woman, and the weariness that was now mingled with the harsh impatience in her voice gave her another facet, another dimension. She was a person, and people had faces that were themselves and gave them reality. Melanie looked at the woman's face.

I know her, came the instant thought in words, came, but as instantly vanished, for Melanie did not know the woman, had never seen her before. She looks about fifty, was the next thought, with the knowledge that the word "looks" was used because the woman was not in fact fifty, but many years younger. She looked older perhaps because her face was uncared for, had never been cared for; or perhaps because her face held no softness of spirit, although it was not cruel, only harsh, hard and unyielding. But it held other softness, softness of bleached flesh that swelled in little bags under the eyes, in puffy cushions round the mouth, in fleshy creases under the chin. Her hair had been black, but it was now streaked with iron-grey, drawn from a centre parting so wide that her head could never have known any other, down over her cheeks in loops like the curtains and then back to a low wide bun. There was something yielding and submissive in those elegant loops of hair, those podgy cushions of protected flesh, that made them altogether inappropriate to the straight thin line of the thin pale chapped lips.

"You'll want your barley water," she said, and she walked swiftly beside Melanie and disappeared behind her head. As she walked, her skirt rustled heavily and then the rustling ceased with a swish as the woman's footsteps stopped and her skirt settled around her. A door was opened and Melanie heard her call, "Lizzie! Lizzie!" An answering voice sounded from far away, but the words were indistinguishable, and then the woman said loudly, "I forgot Miss Milly's barley water. Bring it please." There was a moment of waiting, and then footsteps climbed heavily up uncarpeted stairs and walked along a passage. "Here you are, Miss Adelaide," said a coarse voice, a servant's voice, and the footsteps retreated and the door was closed again.

I must wake up before I see her again, said Melanie urgently inside her head, and she closed her eyes, believing that awareness would instantly fade and, after the timelessness of sleep, her eyes open again to the the sun in the window and the flower-spangled briar. Sleep, sleep, she pleaded, but the thread of awareness held taut, and she could not but hear the footsteps that moved near her again, slow, heavy, enveloped in the heavy swishing of the long skirts, that could not be the brisk steps of Sister Smith set to the faint sussuration of her starched gingham. A glass was set down on the tatted cover of the small round table by her head — How do I know it's a tatted cover, a small round table? cried Melanie to herself, and she must open her eyes, and by her head was the glass tumbler on the tatted cover on the small round table, and beside it still stood the woman.

"There's your barley water," she said in the coarse flat voice Melanie knew — or remembered from the time she had spoken before? "Mr. Endworthy said that he might call before the meeting, and so I'll go and make myself tidy." She half turned, then looked back at Melanie, and spoke with obvious embarrassment. "Do you want — ?" she hesitated, " — do you want anything before I go?"

Melanie shook her head. She had spoken once, but

involuntarily, certain of the transcience of the dream. But an answer was a link, an answer implied a bond of understanding between herself and the creature who stood waiting. So she shook her head, because there was nothing she wanted but to wake up, and as soon as she was alone she could easily, surely easily, sleep and then wake again.

The woman gave a little hitch, barely a shrug of her shoulders. "Don't forget Mr. Endworthy may be coming," she said, and again she walked to the door and turned the handle, and this time, when it closed, Melanie knew she was alone in the room.

Now to sleep, she said, sleep, sleep, sleep, her eyes closed, but her mind still alive. Funny about the table, said her brain, I must have dreamt of here before and forgotten, why the filthy smell still, they say you can't dream colours but I've not dreamt smell before, it's probably the canal and the hot day and the smell got into my room — anyway, said the tiring brain, I do dream colours, I dreamt Adelaide's brooch, the horrid red-brown like poor meat, I've always hated that brooch, it was Gilbert who said it looked like meat, not Adelaide, he wouldn't be so impolite, those brooches ladies are wearing now, he said, you're really getting better, he said, you're really getting better, he said, said Guy and Gilbert, today it was or a long time ago when I could walk and go out, not shut in with the smell of nasty meat, the brown meat and the brown fog and the pain that makes me cough with a rough rough cough which don't rhyme but ought to, blankets pale and grey and rough, tuck my hands in a little grey muff, puff away, puff, little grey muff — and Melanie's conscious brain had relaxed its control and she slept or dozed, and once she opened her eyes, seeing, or thinking she saw, the open window and through it the blue sky and the briar, and rustling away through the door she heard Sister Smith's starched skirt, and again she closed her eyes, whether really or as part of her dream, but safely now, sleeping and all her brain asleep.

Slowly it awoke, an it awoke first to knowledge of the same foetid smell. Still there! said the nose to the brain, and instantaneously Melanie was awake and her eyes open.

Shrunk with fear, she saw the room she was in.

She had turned over in her sleep, and, knowing the lace-hung plush-draped window to be away to her right, she saw beyond her couch's foot a round black iron fireplace, and in its empty hearth a pink paper fan. Over it was a brown wooden mantel, built up with little pillars, little mirrors, till it rose almost to the ceiling. Melanie's gaze passed beyond it, up to the ceiling papered with huge white formalised flowers patterned in smooth and shiny paper; one way the petals seemed shiny, the background smooth, and, the angle of the gaze changing ever so slightly, it was the petals that were smooth and the background gleaming. Melanie looked down again to the over-mantel, which carried so many small objects that she had only a confused impression of worthless trash, brown photographs in clumsy silver or plush frames, two painted vases with bulrushes stuck in them, a bulbous urn plastered over with postage stamps, two ebony elephants, a chased brass bell — it's familiar, I know it, know it all, said Melanie, but her thudding brain could only observe, not comment or deduce. She looked at the heavy red wallpaper, patterned like the ceiling in textures that formed shapes and then shifted as she looked, at the clumsy black chair on the opposite side of the fireplace, its arms and back and seat padded in embossed green velvet that was studded with dull brass nails. One by one she saw the objects in the room, the black squat fire scuttle with its shovel in a slot behind, the round table in the window bay covered with a bobble-fringed green plush cloth, the text in its rustic-wood frame on the wall by the overmantel, reading, in hand-drawn Gothic letters — could she read it, or did she know that it read *GOD BLESS OUR HOME?* From the text she looked down to the carpet, dirty scarlet background and heavy ugly pattern in black and green and a vivid electric blue; then up again to the known round table covered with tatting, the coarse tumbler filled with barley water, and what was behind her head was invisible but known to be the heavy brown-stained door, and now there were only those things close to herself left to observe, the things that clothed and supported and touched her.

But to notice these things, to bring observation so close to herself who lay or seemed to lie there, was not yet possible. Again she looked at the conglomeration of crowded, tasteless, worthless objects on the overmantel, and now the comment came that these were junk, what you'd see in a junk shop, a real junk shop, jostled in an open tray on the pavement on Saturday morning, anything for half a crown. "You won't find anything there," he said, amused and loving, and she half played the foolish little woman, the man knowing better, but she still pleading for her charming little feminine-childish ways. "Just let me look," she begged. "You never know — there just may be something — " and she gazed up at him, miming the playful but obedient kitten. "Please, Guy," she begged, "please, Guy — " and to Melanie looking at the overmantel came full terrible horror, and she screamed aloud: "Guy! Guy!" — and again, gasping in hysterical panic: "Guy! Guy!" She coughed, and choked with coughing, and stopped to call, "Guy, Guy, Guy!" and choked again, and screamed again.

The footsteps came swiftly, down the stairs, along the hall, the handle violently turned, the woman sweeping into the room, to stand, erect and menacing, by her head. "Is that his name?" she panted, her eyes

glittering, fixed horribly on Melanie's face. Venom-
ously, full of menace, she repeated, "Is that his
name?" demanding, insisting upon an answer.

To Melanie, choking and screaming on the sofa,
there came a new dread, or an old fear long known
and endured, of the purple-faced woman who stood
quivering above her. Coughing, coughing until she
choked, was the only protection, and Melanie stopped
screaming for Guy to come and wake her, come and
save her, and dropped her chin on her breast, choking
and gasping for breath.

"Stop it!" commanded the woman. "Stop it and
answer me!"

But Melanie could not stop. The breath would not
come; it was not possible to breathe. Tears broke
from her closed lids, her body shook, and before the
vision of her brain there was only a blood-red blur.

"You must stop," said the woman, not imperiously
now, but with a weary — could it be tenderness?
Hands were pressing on Melanie's shoulders, forcing
her head back against the pillow, letting air again into
the choked windpipe. One hand shifted a little, and
its flesh brushed Melanie's neck.

It was real, that touch of flesh. There was no conceivable atmosphere of dream of which that touch of
rough dry flesh could be a part. Melanie's cough had
stopped, and she opened her eyes and looked into
the woman's. "You are here," Melanie said, "and I
am here, not there. This is real — how can it be

real?" Her jaw clenched, she stared at the dark brown eyes, insisting, as the woman herself had just insisted, upon an answer.

But the woman did not respond as Melanie had, did not recognise urgency and then match it or evade it. "Of course we're both here," she said, straightening herself, and then she bent again and put a hand on Melanie's forehead with a tenderness obviously unpractised, for the hand fell too heavily, and was too rough in its rough mitten to soothe as it moved awkwardly to and fro. Melanie shuddered under its movement and quickly it was withdrawn. She looked up into eyes that now held something of — was it pain at the rebuff? — something at all events that made Melanie bite back the instinctive "Don't touch me." She is as real as I am, she knew, and wondered wildly, How can I be here? "Have I been kidnapped?" she said slowly, staring into the eyes, willing an answer.

"You couldn't have been," said the woman quickly. "That won't do for a story. Whatever you did, you did of your own free will, deceiving me, abusing my trust." She half turned away, and her voice grew thick with emotion. "Milly, I believed every word you said. I thought I knew where you were every minute of the day, and all the while you were deceiving me."

"You're mad," said Melanie, thinking quickly, That's what she is, mad, somehow she's kidnapped me, why doesn't Guy come and find me, save me, take me away?

The woman gave a harsh, broken laugh. "I'm not the one that's mad, my lady," she said, and then in a voice of utter weariness and despair, "Oh, Milly, Milly, why won't you be open and true with me?"

"Why do you call me Milly?" whispered Melanie, thinking, Perhaps this is the explanation, she lives somewhere near, perhaps the slums at the back, she heard Guy calling me Melly one day, and someone she knew, someone called Milly, had died, and so perhaps she came — but where was Sister Smith? she cried despairingly to herself, and how could she get into the house, the front door's never left open, Nanny's so frightened of burglars. But it must be what happened, she told herself, as the woman answered, "What else should I call you, Milly Baines? Not but what I wouldn't thank God on my bended knees if there was another name I could give."

"What name?" asked Melanie. "What name would you thank God for?" She's a religious maniac, she told herself, I must be careful, Guy will be looking for me, he will surely come soon.

"Only you can answer that," said the woman sternly, and then, with that little hitch of the shoulders again, she turned away and sat in the chair by the fire, her arms along its arms, her back rigid, not touching its back.

There was a knock at the door. "Come in," said

the woman, and from behind her head there passed into Melanie's vision another woman, a clumsily stepping woman in a black stuff dress that, like the other's, went right down to the ground. But this woman wore over her dress an oval white apron with a bib rising over her curiously rounded bosom, its top held with a pin, and on her untidy grey hair a flat white band of embroidered cotton with lappets hanging down over her ears. She looks like an old-fashioned maid, came into Melanie's mind, and this woman said in an Irish voice, "Shall it be the plum cake today, Miss Adelaide, since it's the Vicar that may be coming?" She *is* a maid, Melanie told herself, not a slum then, just a madhouse, all of them mad. She heard the first woman answer, "Yes, the plum cake, Lizzie — and, Lizzie — " She rose and jerked her head towards the door, and the maid, understanding, moved away, behind Melanie's head, and the first woman joined her. The door was still open and perhaps they stood just inside it, for all Melanie could hear was the sharp frush-frush of whispering. "What are you saying?" she called involuntarily. Why hadn't the maid been surprised to see her, was she mad too? No, paid, surely paid to show no surprise, to be in the plot. Melanie heard the door close, and then the first woman came back and sat again rigidly in the chair by the fire. "I was only instructing Lizzie to walk round to Dr. Blundell and ask if he could call to see you."

If she's mad enough to get a doctor, thought Melanie, in a flood of relief, then everything will be all right. I've only got to keep her quiet till he comes, and then, whatever kind of a doctor he is, he'll get me out of here. "I think that's a very good idea," she said aloud. "Thank you, Miss Adelaide."

The woman turned her head sharply. "There is no call to mock me," she said. "You may have behaved like a servant girl — " again Melanie noticed the strange pronunciation, gal or gairl — "but there's no need to talk like one." Her voice quickened, as if anger was growing in her. "A fine way to address your sister, I must say."

Melanie thought, I mustn't get her angry. Whatever happens I must keep her calm. Whoever she thinks I am, there is a queer mixture in her feelings towards me, something making her feel angry, something making her feel sorry. "I am sorry, Adelaide," she said, and then wondered why she had said "I am" and not the natural "I'm."

"I accept your apology," said Adelaide, her voice slower and calmer again, and though she still sat rigidly upright in the chair, it seemed to Melanie that this was the way it was natural for her to sit, and not the deliberate effort it seemed to entail. If only I knew what it was all about, I could make party conversation, thought Melanie, but it's hard to know what would be safe, what I can ask and what I'm supposed to know. I made a bad bloomer calling her

45

Miss Adelaide; fancy being sister to a creature like that.

For lack of anything to say, she stared again at the overpowering mantelshelf with its heavy cargo, looking from elephant to brass pot, from bulrushes to glass urn, from the brown photograph in the fat silver frame on the right to the brown photograph in the faded velvet frame on the left. Lizzie must have changed them over, she heard her mind saying, it always used to be Aunt Carrie on the left, and, in sudden despair, I'm going mad myself, how the hell do I know whose photographs they are? And then the other voice, with confident menace, But I do know, I do. It used to be Aunt Carrie on the left and Uncle George on the right, and now it is the other way round.

"Adelaide," she said sharply, "those portraits on the mantelshelf. Have not they been changed over? Was not Uncle George on the other side yesterday?"

It must be, it can only be thoughts passing from her mind to mine, she told herself. For Adelaide stood up, showing no surprise at the question, and peered sharply at the photographs, first at one, then at the other.

She turned to Melanie. "You are right," she said, and then she turned back and reversed the photographs, blowing a speck of dust off the silver frame as she did so. "Lizzie must have changed them when

46

she dusted," she said, and, irritably, "It seems impossible to find a girl who will take the trouble to remember exactly how I like my things to be kept."

I must find something new to say, thought Melanie, it must be safer when she is talking than sitting there so silently and menacingly — and if I don't think of something to say for myself, perhaps still more thoughts will come from her mind into mine, and that must not happen. I must keep my mind to myself.

Oh Guy, Guy, she cried to herself, come, come and save me, come quickly, it is getting to be so long — it must be a long time now, she thought, and, schooling her voice carefully, she asked, "Adelaide, what is the time?"

"It must be nearly two o'clock," said Adelaide, running her finger speculatively over the whorls on the pillars, licking a finger and then rubbing it on the wood to see whether it picked up any dust.

"But it cannot be!" Melanie exclaimed. It was after two when Guy had gone back to chambers. Surely — no, they could not have drugged her, it could not be that days had passed and she was still lost and unrescued. What was the date? she worried, April the — I know it was just after Summer Time — yesterday was the Queen's birthday, it was that programme just before the news — it must be the twenty-second, then. If I ask, perhaps she'll lie, but why should she, she's so dotty, she won't know why I'm asking. "Adelaide," she said, "what is the date today?"

"April the twenty-second," said Adelaide.

Then it *is* still today, thought Melanie, but to be sure she repeated questioningly, "The twenty-second?"

Adelaide said wearily, "The twenty-second of April, eighteen hundred and sixty-four."

For an instant, for ever, Melanie was bound in timeless fear. Her eyes were forced open, rigid and unblinking, her mouth hung open, the rigid lips stretched in a terrible grin, all her being was rigid with unimaginable terror. For she knew that this was true.

As slowly as the passing of rigor after death, the bonds began to loosen and the brain to flutter. There was nothing yet she could think or feel or do; only from her mouth there came incoherent dribbling whimperings.

Adelaide came swiftly to the couch. "What is it?" she asked. "Are you in pain?" and, aloud but to herself, "Let us pray that Dr. Blundell comes soon. What is it, Milly?" she repeated, and Melanie saw the mittened hand holding the tumbler to her lips. "Try a sip," said Adelaide, "only a sip."

"No," moaned Melanie, "no," clenching her teeth tightly, shaking her head to move it away from the proffered draught. More powerful than any reason, an overwhelming passion of disgust told her that this body must not be nourished, not linked by nourishment to water long since tainted and drained away. "I am recovered," she whispered, "truly, Adelaide, it was only a momentary spasm." There seemed to be no control over the words that came to phrase her mental intentions: they were alien words and phrases, yet no more deliberately chosen than any words one ordinarily chooses to frame a thought. "If I could be alone for a little," she whispered, "only for a little."

Adelaide straightened and watched her for an instant, frowning. It was clear that she could act only on her own initiative, never admitting that a suggestion or a request had been made. "I must give out the Madeira cloth," she pronounced, but a little uncertainly. "I will give you the bell," she said with more assurance, and from the clutter on the mantelshelf she picked up the chased brass bell, Brummagem ware from India, the cherished souvenir. "There," she said, setting it on the tatting beside the rejected tumbler. "Do not hesitate to ring if you should feel the least suspicion faint or — or strange — " she finished, her voice rising as if herself surprised at the last word. Melanie closed her eyes and listened, first to the silence as Adelaide stood there uncertainly, then to the rustling of the skirt, the opening and at last the closing of the door.

And then she opened her eyes and lay for a moment quiescent, drained of all will and feeling by the power of her unspeakable knowledge. The fluttering,

49

the thundering in her brain, her breast, her stomach were too overwhelming to allow thought, but not for an instant could there by any evasion of the truth and reality that she was here.

"Why?" she said at last, and she said it aloud.

Now, slowly and fitfully, she began to wonder.

I am awake but I cannot be awake, she said to herself, and between each statement she made, there was a pause, long, and then shorter, of horrible convulsive trembling. I know Adelaide, I know this room — but queerly, like half remembering last night's dream just before going to sleep. Does one know in a dream that one's dreaming? Sometimes — yes, and then one longs to wake, struggles to wake, and that is just before waking. But I have been struggling to wake for so long. I know I am really asleep and I know this is real, as real as home. Adelaide is as real as Guy — but Guy is *my* reality. Here I can smell and see and think and feel, as much as I really can. Only I can't remember properly, all my memory is with Guy — that makes this not so real, she said doubtfully, and then, That must make this not so real. Anyway, she said, and she tried to say it aloud, but the words would not form on the air, only in her brain, I am Melanie Langdon. I am not this Milly Baines, oh no, I am not Milly Baines — and the power of this cry, silent though it was, exhausted her thoughts again, and again the terrified fluttering in her body swelled and drowned her.

Who is Milly Baines? came the gradual inquiry, and at last she looked, as she had not dared to before, at what was immediately around her, examined, tested, interpreted the feeling of this body of Milly Baines in which was imprisoned the brain of Melanie Langdon.

It was lying down, this body, in less than comfort, on a stiff bumpy hardness that was, perhaps, the cause of the aching back. Over the body there was a grey knitted blanket or rug edged with long fringes of its own harsh grey wool. The head lay on a soft pillow or cushion; Melanie turned her head to see what it lay on — not lifted it, that seemed too hard to do, only turned it, and even that was hard. The head lay on a square pillow in a white linen case round whose edge jutted stiff goffered frills. With difficulty, Melanie rolled her head back again, and for a moment had to stop looking while dizziness overcame her, rocked her with nausea and died away. A hand lay on the grey coverlet, an arm in a thick white cotton sleeve that was caught in tightly at the wrist and then edged with a stiff frill, like the frill on the pillow. A hand — and beside it another hand. I don't like her hands, whispered Melanie to herself, and as she thought this, she slowly lifted one hand, the right hand, scratching up the wine-red felt, over the embroidered roses up to the carved wooden frame of the back of the Victorian chaise longue.

And in the instant before she had perceived what

she was touching, she was flooded with that same memory that had stirred in her when she first saw the chaise longue in the shop off Marylebone High Street, only now it was deeper, truer, and intolerably painful, a memory of passionate love, of a body that crushed and broke into hers, pressed down on the Victorian chase longue.

So that's it, she said, not understanding the memory, only recognising that this thing, this couch on which she lay, was the only object that joined that life and this. There was a pattern: it was not all haphazard. If I could get off it then, she thought, and she dug her elbows into the horsehair-filled seat and lifted the swimming dizzy head.

She could raise her head — but not for long. Before she could tell the unseen legs that they must move too, move away from their foul disastrous nest, she fell back on the pillow, her head thudding emptily as though it had been hit very hard, her heart beating with great pulsations not only in her breast but all over her body, with huge destructive thuds.

Then she thought, But when I was not on the chaise longue, I was there. If I get off it, perhaps I shall be here, irrevocably here. If I lie still and wait, surely soon I shall go back. I can't stay here, she cried to herself, I can't be lost here, and die here.

She said, Perhaps Milly Baines died here. Then — Milly Baines must surely be dead now, she said blankly, Milly and Adelaide and Lizzie, all dead and rotten long ago. This body I am in, it must have rotted filthily, this pillowcase must be a tatter of rag, the coverlet corrupt with moth, crisp and sticky with matted moths' eggs, falling away into dirty crumbling scraps. It's all dead and rotten, the barley water tainted, the nightgown threadbare and thrown away, these hands, all this body stinking, rotten, dead. She shuddered, and knew she was shuddering in a body long ago dead. Her flesh crawled away, and it was flesh that had turned green and liquescent and at last become damp dust with the damp crumbling coffin wood.

And as she lay there in a fever of disgust at all she was, all she seemed to be, this body, this foul unreal body, began to make its demands on her. I can't, she cried voicelessly, I can't. This cannot feel and want and have needs like mine, it would be disgusting beyond everything that these long decayed organs should need what real bodies need. If I let it have needs, it becomes mine. I pass what is decayed and horrible, pass it from a rotten filthy dead dead body. But the need grew and grew, till it became overwhelming, till it became greater than the disgust which, although not itself vanishing, became mingled with disgust of a different kind, the disgust of embarrassment, so often felt yet never diminished, at what must be done.

Melanie lifted her left hand, slowly and with difficulty, and twitched the brass bell from off the tatting. She shook it rather by the action of pulling it off the table than by any deliberate shaking; the bell seemed too heavy for that, too heavy, too, to replace, so that when Adelaide came into the room, the bell was lying on the coverlet, loosely held by Melanie's weak fingers.

"Well?" asked Adelaide, and bent over and replaced the bell upright on the tatting beside the tumbler.

"I want — " began Melanie, "I want — I am afraid that I must — " She was choking with shame, and could not go on.

Adelaide sighed. "It is barely half an hour since I asked you, and you said no," she complained, but, before she had finished speaking, she had gone to the fireplace to take a box of matches from a pink and white china mug on the mantelshelf. She took out a match and struck it, and it burned with a bright blue flame and much smoke that smelt strongly of sulphur. Adelaide wrinkled her nose and held the match well away from her until the blue flame had changed into an orange one when the smoke and the sulphurous smell died away. As Adelaide turned her back, lifting the match, Melanie saw on each side of the overmantel a gas bracket jutting from an elaborately curled brass arm. Adelaide lit only the one on the left-hand side, and it burned with a sharp hiss from a flame shaped like a quivering heart.

The matches were replaced in the china mug, and

Adelaide went to the window and pulled the heavy plush curtains over the heavy greyed lace, leaving no chink for the foggy daylight to penetrate. Melanie's need became increasingly urgent. She could hardly endure the slow deliberate steps that took Adelaide, first to the door behind Melanie's head to turn the key in the lock, and then to the double doors that faced the windows with crimson plush bobble-fringed curtains looped over their frame. Adelaide opened one of these doors and went through into the room beyond.

Through the gap left by the opened door, Melanie could see that this room was a bedroom with walls papered in stripes of vivid ugly flowers. Its head against the far wall, there stood a high black iron bedstead. High iron posts at its head, with short truncated rails jutting from them, carried pink stuff curtains that seemed to be caught back with their ends, instead of falling to the ground, laid across the bolster. To the right, Melanie could see the corner of what appeared to be a white marble washstand top, and here Adelaide disappeared from view, returning soon through the double doors, carrying, under a white cloth, a chamber pot.

The next minutes were darkened by blinding embarrassment. These actions, although so many times performed, were intolerable to both women, and when they were over, and Adelaide had carried away the chamber pot, covered again by its decorous cloth,

Melanie was lying back distraught and with her eyes shut, trying to blot out not the constant nightmare but the memory of shame beyond anything she had ever felt or conceived.

She heard Adelaide empty the chamber pot and swill it out. She heard her pour out water, wash her own hands, and throw that water away too. She heard her come back into the room, shut the double door, turn out the gas, which died with a full sighing plop, heard her draw back the window draperies with the now remembered and recognisable squeaking drag of the rings on their mahogany rod. The light struck Melanie's lids again, but she could not open her eyes and meet Adelaide's, who had unlocked the door to the hall and called, "Lizzie! The lavender shovel!"

There was a moment's waiting, and then Lizzie's heavy steps came up the stone stairs, along the passage and into the room. Now curiosity forced open Melanie's eyes, and she saw Lizzie come past her couch, holding at arm's length a black kitchen shovel on which burned red embers.

Adelaide was standing by the fireplace, a small green bottle in her hand. Lizzie held out the shovel to her, and on the embers Adelaide dripped liquid from the bottle. There was a sizzling, and smoke rose from the shovel, heavy with the smell of lavender. Adelaide recorked the bottle, and replaced it behind the jar containing the bulrushes, while Lizzie walked about the room, holding the shovel before her, waving it slowly from side to side.

The embers were nearly grey when she again passed by the couch on her way out of the room. "You had best lay the table now, Lizzie," said Adelaide, and Lizzie said, "Yes, Miss Adelaide," and went out of the room.

Without thinking, Melanie put out a wavering hand and took the glass off the table, and sipped the barley water. It was thick and slightly warm, but soothing to her throat that had been so long parched with fear. As she sipped, she realised that she was indeed succouring this body in which she lay, nourishing the tissues that seemed so strangely to be bearing her living brain, but still she went on sipping. To drink was of the same order of actions as to pass water. The accomplishment of the one had perhaps been the act of committal she dreaded; if so, then drinking could in no wise bind her more closely, and drinking slightly soothed and relaxed her torn nerves together with her dry throat.

For there must be a way out, she told herself. Not getting off the chaise longue, that I daren't try, not going to sleep, I tried that and it didn't work — or did it? she wondered desperately. Didn't I go back when I was asleep, didn't I see the window and hear Sister Smith rustling round the room? Or did *she* go, this Milly — oh no, she can't be there instead of me,

57

not her, in my body, Guy bending over her and loving her instead of me. She was pierced with jealousy, seeing Guy with another woman, forgetting her, his Melanie, never even knowing that she had gone. Or perhaps she's frightened too, she said, twisting the knife in the wound, and Guy is reassuring her, just thinking she's had a nightmare, then liking her better than me, oh, she'd be all right with Guy, anyone would, not here with the dead, with this cruel hard Adelaide, oh, she wept to herself, I can't be left here, it's so lonely, so frightening, oh Guy — but this time she knew better than to cry aloud, only closed her eyes, and hot tears welled from under her eyelids, another thing this body could do, this body of Milly's, to weep for Melanie's misery.

Adelaide was wiping the tears from her eyes, roughly and impatiently, "Pull yourself together, Milly," she said. "Lizzie is coming with the cloth."

Melanie sighed, and did, as Adelaide demanded, pull herself together. There was no relief to be found in surrender, in succumbing to the utter loneliness and terror of the past. Somehow she must master it, summon all knowledge she had ever had, all instinct she had ever owned, if she was to escape. "Heaven helps those that help themselves," she said aloud, traditional succour that came as she called for it. "Very true," said Adelaide, sitting down in her usual seat, as Lizzie came up with the lace-encrusted tea cloth.

She went over to the table by the window and spread the cloth carefully over the fringed green plush that already covered the table. To and fro she came and went, bringing the silver tea service on the japanned tray, the plum cake on the lace mat on the gold-rimmed white platter, the biscuits in their china jar, the split scones, the white bread and butter, the strawberry jam in the shell-shaped china dish, the ivory-handled tea knives, the apostle spoons. "You have got the cloth rucked up," Adelaide called sharply, and, "Not the spoon *in* the jam; take it away and wash it, and then lay it on the cloth *beside* the jam."

"Adelaide," said Melanie cautiously, as Lizzie, after one of the invariable "Yes, Miss Adelaide's" that followed the continual correction, went back for still another load for the table, she wondered, and rehearsed her opening as "please tell me — " would that sound strange? "please tell me again about this chaise longue."

"Again?" commented Adelaide, looking towards her, "I can hardly tell you again, since, so far as I am aware, you have never asked me about it before."

"Have I not?" said Melanie, surprised. Then I don't share Milly's memory, she told herself, it was my own mind wondering whether I should say "again" or not. "Please tell me now, Adelaide," she begged.

"One minute," said Adelaide. Lizzie had just placed the cut currant loaf on the table, and was on her way back to the door. "Lizzie," she said, "you did not tell me what they said at Dr. Blundell's when you called there."

Lizzie stopped just by the back of the couch. "There now," she said. "Be forgetting my own head if it was loose," and she smacked the side of her head in a gesture of mock anger.

Nanny does that, thought Melanie with a stab of recognition, that's what Nanny says, and she jerked her head upwards to stare at Lizzie, searching passionately for a likeness, an identity, that would bring pattern and sense into chaos. "He's gone to Richmond, their Annie said," Lizzie explained, "for to see Sir John. Missus didn't know when he'd be back, she said, but she'd ask him to call round, she said."

"Thank you, Lizzie," said Adelaide. Lizzie drooped quickly and then up again in something less than a bob, and went out of the room, this time closing the door behind her. No, there was no resemblance Melanie could be sure of. This woman was younger — but did she have to be the same age? — they both had blue eyes, but the clothes, the hair made such a difference; Melanie was almost sure there was no resemblance.

"What was I saying?" asked Adelaide absently. "Oh yes, of course, about the chaise longue." This will be the revelation, Melanie told herself, looking above all for the shape, the pattern, the proved way here that would be the way back again. But it was hard even to understand the story that Adelaide told, because it was told to a listener who knew its background, and to Melanie it must be like a story overheard in a tea shop, words with meaning, but no shape save to the intended hearer who could herself people the gaps that reflected mutual knowledge.

"It was Uncle Edward," said Adelaide. "That was in the Chalk Farm days, of course, and I do not remember myself, but dear Mother told me that day at Bognor. They were not so comfortable then, times being hard for everyone and very little doing at Smithfield. Even a loaf of bread cost I don't know how much, but it was a great deal of money. Not that we ever wanted for bread, but there was nothing to spare for titbits, and dear Mother did not find the armchairs satisfactory." Adelaide lowered her voice. "Her poor *legs* were swollen, but to ask for a sofa would hardly have been right. Dear Mother was always so loyal." She looked up from her mittened hands, reproachfully and accusingly at Melanie. Melanie was bewildered. Surely it should have been Uncle George, not Uncle Edward? Uncle Edward was a new character, no part of the pattern. And who was at Smithfield? Was that Uncle Edward, or was it dear Mother's husband? Was he a butcher? — no, at Smithfield he would be a wholesaler, a wholesale butcher — yes, that was right. Melanie was sure that was right. That was Adelaide, the daughter of a prosperous tradesman. And was that Milly too?

"Of course Uncle Edward would never have *said* anything," continued Adelaide in a shocked tone, looking down at her hands again. "It was Cousin Dora who gave the sofa, but dear Mother knew that Uncle had noticed. It was covered in black horsehair when it first came, and dear Mother told me, jokingly of course, that, grateful as she was, she was always afraid she might slip off it in company, and when she laid me on it in the cashmere shawl, she would put a chair at the side to be sure I did not roll over onto the floor."

"That was a sensible thing to do," commented Melanie. There had been a pause in the story, and a comment was clearly expected.

"Dear Mother was not always so provident, I fear," said Adelaide with a sigh. It was obvious that Milly, too, should sigh and share the regret. "I sometimes wonder — " Adelaide began, and checked herself. "No, that would not be right. Besides, one must not judge. He was sorely tried, too."

"About the chaise longue, Adelaide," put in Melanie timidly.

"It was when — " Adelaide coughed. "It was before you were born," she said with obvious courage. "Dear Mother was determined that this time she would have some comfort after her lying-in, and, of course, by that time she could pick and choose within reason. Papa had bought the green sofa when we moved to Clapham, but it went straight into the smoking room, and I know she didn't like to ask. Mind you, it was more comfortable with the plush, but there were Uncle Edward's feelings to consider as well. So she did the embroidery herself while she waited, and left it all ready, and Mr. Tuppitt came — *young* Mr. Tuppitt he was then — and upholstered it the very day after you were born. I well remember him carrying her downstairs — " Not Mr. Tuppitt, surely, wondered Melanie. "— and settling her on the new sofa, as we called it for quite a time. It must have been a Sunday, or he would have been at Smith-field — " *Not* Mr. Tuppitt, then, Melanie decided. " — or wait, had he retired then?" Adelaide put her hand to her brow, pondering. "No, it was a Sunday, for I remember Cook and the girl coming in to evening prayers, and the monthly nurse brought you down too, so that you might, Papa said, be one with us in our prayers from the very commencement of your life. Yes, he offered up a special prayer for you that evening. And now *you* lie there!" cried Adelaide suddenly, and she thrust towards Melanie a menacing forefinger. "Thank God, thank God they are dead," she cried, and she buried her face in her hands.

Melanie heard the coarse gulping sobs with cold repulsion. The story had been useless. Momentarily she even forgot why she had asked for it, as she thought that she would never have bought the thing if she had known the kind of background it had, this vulgar tradesman's family, the reticences, the hints,

Mother's legs and Chalk Farm and Clapham. Then is *this* Clapham? suddenly occurred to her, I'd assumed it was our house, no, not our house, the rooms are different, bigger, and this is a ground floor, not a first floor, and Victorian, not Regency. "Is this Clapham?" she asked aloud, but Adelaide acknowledged the question only with an angry twitch of her body and continued sobs.

But it must have been the chaise longue, argued Melanie. There is no other link; something to do with Milly and the chaise longue that was so powerful, that even I in the present, just by lying on it, couldn't help but feel it. Of course I'm in the present, she maintained, in the real present I'm asleep on the chaise longue at home, Sister Smith creeping in and then out again because I'm still sleeping. This, which seems like time, must be instantaneous, without duration or reality. But I seem real to Adelaide, she pondered; did what is happening now happen then, with Milly, or is it different because I am here? But Adelaide can only have lived once. Either this happened with Milly or with me. And if it happened with Milly, then Milly *is* me, or was me, Milly lying here must have been to the future, my present, and it must have happened before the past. Then is it over and done with, no more future to come, or did Milly wait — ? But however long she waited, she must have died before Guy was born, never seen Guy, never known him, or else the knowing Guy is already over,

over for ever. It's not real enough for that, it can't be, she cried to herself, only a dream that never happened, perhaps an instant of reality, Adelaide and Milly and I in Milly's brain, and the rest only imaginings in sleep. There must be a way to get back with this never having happened — and rigidly intense, her lips were drawn back in a horrible convulsive grin, Adelaide still weeping noisily in her chair, Melanie once more rigid in fear.

Outside the window a gate clicked and footsteps crunched on gravel. "Mr. Endworthy!" said Milly sharply. "Adelaide, I hear Mr. Endworthy."

As she had anticipated, Adelaide, while the footsteps climbed up the stone steps, swiftly straightened her shoulders, found a handkerchief tucked under her bodice at the waist, scrubbed at her eyes, patted her hair. "Knock and Ring" must have run a notice on the door, for a heavy knocker thumped commandingly, and soon afterwards the bell rang down in the basement, a heavy bell shaking from the pull on its wire. Adelaide was standing before her chair, the last strangled sobs subsiding into heavy breathing as Lizzie's footsteps climbed the basement stairs and clumped along the hall.

"Good afternoon," said Mr. Endworthy in the hall, "Miss Baines is at home?" and hearing the slow, cultured voice, hope leapt in Melanie. He is obviously an educated man, she thought, if I can make him understand, he will know what to do. He is a clergyman, he can pray, and it will be all right, in the stories ghosts always go when you pray, I could pray myself, she thought, hearing the umbrella slither into the stand, the arrangements for the hat and the overcoat and the galoshes, but it would be better to wait, of course it would work if I prayed myself and I do believe in Him — meticulously thrusting away the name of God that might itself be a prayer that in the saying proved inefficacious — but it would be better to let a clergyman do it, then nothing can go wrong. And when I get back, she thought (for of course the bargain must be made) I will be properly religious, not just Christmas, after all, I was christened and confirmed, I was married in church, and religion — why, the reason for religion, the only reason for religion is that it can make you, keep you safe. If religion weren't true, then there would be no salvation, no comfort for being alive and alone, there would be nothing but living and dying — no, that cannot be so, she said aghast, that could not be endured, of course religion is true and will save me, confident at last that here was the key, the one magic that could not fail. "Mr. Endworthy, miss," said Lizzie's voice as the door opened and the clergyman came in, past Melanie's couch, to shake the hand Adelaide held out to him.

"Mr. Endworthy," cried Melanie, breaking into the conventional greetings between the one and the other. "Mr. Endworthy, I must speak to you alone. It is important."

"Milly!" exclaimed Adelaide in outraged rebuke, and Mr. Endworthy dropped Adelaide's hand and turned towards the chaise longue.

Yes, he'll do, Melanie told herself, her giddy head lifted tensely from the pillow, inspecting him. This was a clergyman who should be able to work miracles by prayer, benign eyes, big authoritative nose, paternal white head. "I am sorry you are not so well today, Miss Milly," he said, and his voice did not rebuke but was tolerant and kind. Shouldn't he know already, Melanie asked herself, should he even call me Miss Milly? Can the pattern be right if he doesn't understand as soon as he sees me? She searched his face for a change, the sign that he had realised and understood, but it was not there. "Oh, I must speak to you immediately," she cried, not knowing what she said in her urgency, and it was still without anger that he replied, "We shall all speak together, I hope, Miss Milly. That is why one comes out to tea, is it not?" and he smiled, but not with understanding, only to soothe.

Behind him Adelaide said again, "Milly!" and then, to the clergyman, "Mr. Endworthy, I am so ashamed. I had hoped that to-day — " She broke off, and then said, with a note of despair, "But one can never be *sure*."

Mr. Endworthy turned back to Adelaide and said graciously, "Do not be perturbed, dear Miss Baines. We must all make allowances for those in sickness or distress, must we not?"

Melanie's head fell back on the pillow. It was silly to expect it all to have happened by now. Time was still theirs, and it was through their pattern she must grope her way. She said weakly, "I am sorry, Adelaide. I am sorry, Mr. Endworthy. I did not mean to be rude, only, Mr. Endworthy, it is imperative that I speak to you alone."

There was something strangely dissimilar about their reactions. "Milly!" Adelaide exclaimed again, but the tone was different, not outrage now, but warning and fear. Mr. Endworthy said gently to Milly, "Do you not think, Miss Milly, that serious conversation could wait until we have done justice to the excellent spread I spy on yonder board?" He smiled down at her quizzically, and unwillingly Melanie smiled back. It was essential to her that Mr. Endworthy should be totally, absolutely right and powerful. If he chose to make little jokes, then it was proper that little jokes should be made. So she smiled and said with attempted lightness. "Indeed I am sorry for my haste." It was hard to smile. She rolled her head painfully on the pillow, and sighed. "It was only," she said, "that I feel such urgent need of spiritual consolation." The words shaped themselves apart from her will, which had wished to speak of desperate need for help. She stopped, puzzled at this discrepancy between her thought and the words her tongue had spoken.

"You shall have it," said Mr. Endworthy. He stepped to the couch, and picked up her hand, pressing it gently in his. Behind him, Melanie could see Adelaide frowning with something more than disapproval, frowning as she moved her lips in a soundless, menacing message that Melanie could not interpret.

Her hand was replaced on the coverlet, and the Vicar turned to Adelaide again. "Shall we refresh the inner man?" he said gaily, and Adelaide summoned Lizzie, not, this time, by shouting from the door, but pressing down the white china handle of a bell beside the fireplace.

"Let me assist," said Mr. Endworthy, and it was he who set the patterned china cup on the small table by Melanie's head, handed the china bowl filled with roughly broken lumps of grey-white sugar, gave to her weak hands a plate on which lay one thin diamond of bread and butter. "No, nothing more, thank you," said Melanie, as he begged her to accept the scones or the biscuits, and at last he desisted, and sat with his back to her at the loaded table in the window.

Melanie folded the bread and butter and tried to eat it. The butter was nasty, oversalt and slightly rancid, seeming to have absorbed some of the room's foul smell of which she was continually aware. But I must eat, she told herself, I must overcome this sick dizziness and feel strong. If this body is dead, I am still, for the moment, imprisoned within it. To eat is not to tie my mind to it, only to nourish the machine it inhabits, to give me strength to struggle and think — but if to think, then my mind *is* tied to this body, my mind *can* be nourished by this food, this rotten, rotted, long-decayed food. She gulped, the bread she had eaten coming back into her mouth in an acrid filthy mess, and she covered her mouth with her hand to smother the noise of her gagging, forced the half-digested lump back into her stomach, for fear that her sick distress might cause Mr. Endworthy to leave, judging the poor invalid unfit for further strain. "They chose the name of Theodore," he was saying to Adelaide, "and I cannot help but feel — " In tiny morsels Melanie ate the bread and butter, and Adelaide, looking up, saw that she had finished, and came to the couch to support Melanie's head with one hand and hold the tea cup to her lips with the other. "Is there anything more I can pass to Miss Milly?" asked Mr. Endworthy, half rising in his seat, and Adelaide wiped Melanie's lips with a little fringed napkin, and answered, "Nothing more, I fear, Mr. Endworthy. My poor sister has the appetite of a mouse now," and, carrying the cup and plate with her, she sat down again at the head of the table. "But Mrs. Brandon," she said, "will hardly be in a position to take the Fancyware again," and the Vicar cocked his head doubtfully and wondered whether, in view of the circumstances, a special effort might not be made.

Their conversation should have been significant, but it was only boring. It was obvious to Melanie that it was not from this drone of timeless platitudes that one clue would shine in unmistakable illumination. The tea had refreshed her, there was no doubt of that, and more, it had allowed her, just a little, to relax. For the first time since her awakening, the taut strings that gathered her flesh into one terrible expectancy had loosened their hold. They should say something I can remember afterwards, she thought in almost amusement, almost annoyance. Instead of talking about these silly women and the weather and the bazaar, they should speak of Queen Victoria and Florence Nightingale and — But what *should* they be talking about? she asked herself. What *did* happen in 1864? Not the Exhibition, of course, and the Crimea must be over. Is the Prince Consort dead? Who is the Prime Minister? Frowning, she thought, But it is I who should know these things. I have got to prove myself to Mr. Endworthy, prove that I really come from the future. I should know what is just going to happen — but what *is?* If I was one of those educated women, she thought angrily, an old resentment, long buried in marriage, rearing its head again. I know what the Victorian age was like, of course I do, except that being here, it isn't like that at all. It's just like now — and she frowned still more deeply, dredg-

ing from her mind a series of phrases — Gladstone
and Disraeli, the First Matabele, Mrs. Bloomer,
Tracts for the Times, landau and brougham — but
none of them could tell Mr. Endworthy what he must
understand. I don't know the dates, she thought, and
even if I did, how can I use them? If I speak of
Cardinal Newman and he's happened already, it
proves nothing at all. If I could say that the Govern-
ment will fall and the Prince Consort will die, there's
no proof it's going to happen. Discoveries and in-
ventions, she thought then, that's what I'll talk about,
that must prove it to him. We have aeroplanes, she
said tentatively in her mind, and then she tried to repeat the phrase soundlessly with her mouth, but the
exact words would not come. What did I say, she
asked herself when the effort had been made, something about machines that fly, or was it aeronautic
machines? Wireless, she screamed in her mind, tele-
vision, penicillin, gramophone records and vacuum
cleaners, but none of these words could be framed by
her lips. I can think them, why can't I say them? she
begged; can I introduce nothing into this real past?
— and if I cannot, then even these thoughts I am
thinking, has Milly thought them before? But things
can't happen twice, she told herself wearily, closing
her eyes, the momentary relaxation over, the racking
torture established again, I must always have been
Milly and Milly me. It is now that is present reality
and the future is still to come. But if I have to wait

for the future, if it is only in time to come that I shall be Melanie again, then that time must come again too when Sister Smith leaves me to sleep on the chaise longue, and I wake up in the past. I shall never escape — and the eternal prison she imagined consumed her mind, and she fainted or dozed off into a nightmare of chase and pursuit and loss.

"Milly has dropped off," said Adelaide with relief in her voice, "so I think that perhaps — "

"I am not asleep," said Melanie wearily. Her eyes were wet with tears again when she opened them to see Adelaide and the Vicar standing beside her couch. She caught at his black frock coat. "Do not go," she entreated, "please do not go until I have spoken with you."

"I did promise Miss Milly," said the Vicar. "So I think, if I may, Miss Adelaide — ? Just a few minutes? I promise not to tire her."

"We had better sit down again, then," said Adelaide with deliberate bad grace, and Melanie, still grasping Mr. Endworthy's coat, threw all she had of passionate entreaty into her eyes.

With a rush of thankfulness she saw the response in his. She let her hand fall from his coat now, at last assured that his understanding was hers. "If you will forgive me, Miss Adelaide," he said gently, "I think I should talk to Miss Milly in privacy."

Adelaide stiffened and said sharply, "Milly has no

secrets from me." Why is she so frightened? Melanie wondered. She doesn't know. I am sure she doesn't know.

"No one who recalls the many sacrifices you have made," said Mr. Endworthy to Adelaide, "can doubt the perfect understanding that exists between you two. But there are times when even sisterly understanding — " He spoke very quietly and Melanie could not properly hear what he said. Was it "a soul and its Maker"? Was it "a soul so near its Maker"? What had Mr. Endworthy said?

"Then I shall leave you, since you insist," said Adelaide, coldly unconvinced. She came past the Vicar to bend over Melanie and adjust her pillow, and, as she bent, Melanie heard, hissed into her ear, "Remember. You promised." Then before Melanie's bewildered eyes could question her, she had swished about and gone, the door closing softly behind her.

To Melanie's surprise, Mr. Endworthy looked at her quickly, then went behind her head to the door. She heard him open it and close it again, heard, as she had not heard when Adelaide shut it, the click of the latch. "These doors do not always shut properly," said Mr. Endworthy as if to himself, coming back past the chaise longue. He set Adelaide's chair beside it, then sat down and took Melanie's hand, still drooping over the side of the couch, between his. "Now what is it?" he said.

It was vital that it should be rightly said, impossi-

ble to know how to begin. Melanie gazed imploringly
into Mr. Endworthy's eyes, and involuntarily she began to tremble. "Now, now," said Mr. Endworthy
gently. She opened her mouth and closed it again,
and the dreadful shivering went on. "There now,"
said Mr. Endworthy, and he pressed her hand sooth-
ingly with his own soft white cushiony sexless hand.
"Try to be calm, my dear," he said. "You will never
tell me what troubles you unless you can calm yourself first."

"But it's so important," Melanie whispered. She
sighed once heavily, needing the breath, and after
that the trembling ceased. "Do you swear you will
believe me?" she asked Mr. Endworthy.

"If you tell me the truth, of course I shall believe
you," he said. Melanie swallowed painfully. "How
long have you known me?" she asked.

Surely that was not a strange question? Why did
he answer as if to a child? "I think you were five
when your dear parents decided to join my congrega-
tion," he said, "and even before that I had noticed
you trotting down the pavements to the Baptist Sunday School between those two big sisters of yours."
He smiled at her kindly. "You were always a very
pretty little girl, Miss Milly."

"*Two* sisters," said Melanie, warmed by his kindness but perplexed by what he had said. There had
been no other sister in the pattern she had deduced,
only Papa and dear Mother and Adelaide. Why

didn't people explain? — but of course you explained nothing to people you knew well, because you knew that they knew already.

The Vicar was frowning slightly. "You are sure you are not too tired to talk now?" he suggested, moving a little in his chair as if he might rise and go away, and Melanie with her free hand caught at his wrist and weakly held him. "No, no," she exclaimed. "You will soon see why I was surprised. Tell me, please, when you last saw me before today."

The Vicar spoke with gentle care. "It was yesterday," he said, "when I brought the cards and you so very kindly said you would letter them for me. I did, indeed, wonder whether it might not prove too much for you, but I know how hard it is to occupy oneself when one has been ill for so long — " He stopped, looking at her closely and doubtfully.

Trying to speak as strongly as she could, Melanie asked, "Do you find me different from yesterday?"

"Do you mean in appearance?" asked Mr. Endworthy. "Or — " and Melanie broke in — it seemed easier to proceed now, as if a sudden access of confidence was upholding her — "I mean in anything — in appearance or speech or character — do I seem to you a different person?"

"You want me to say yes," said Mr. Endworthy. "Why do you want that?"

"I want the truth," said Melanie. "You must tell me — Am I different?"

The Vicar hesitated. "It is an impossible question to answer," he said. "I do not know what difference you want me to look for. You seem perhaps less languid than yesterday — " he checked himself. "No, that is true now, but it was certainly not true when we were taking our tea. Perhaps the change you speak of is a spiritual one?" He leant forward, gazing into her eyes, and spoke with authority. "Come, Miss Milly, what have you in mind to say to me?"

Melanie said with great difficulty, each word a pain, "I am not really Milly Baines."

Mr. Endworthy said nothing, only continued to gaze at her.

"I do not belong here," said Melanie. "I come from the future. I am married, happily married. I have a child — " Mr. Endworthy groaned, his face distorted with pain. She held on to his wrist convulsively, and her words poured out. "I went to sleep on the sofa, this sofa, and I woke up here. I have never been here before. I have never seen you before. I don't know this room or this house. I don't belong here. I want to go back." For the first time, she sat up, still clutching his hand. "Mr. Endworthy, you must help me to go back."

"Lie down, lie down," he said quickly. He disengaged his hand from hers and stood up, gently forcing her back against the pillow. "I — I — " he stammered, and before he could make that move to the door she had divined was in his mind, she was speaking quickly, urgently, imploringly, while he stood beside the couch, distraught, looking down at her.

"You think I am Milly Baines gone mad," she said, "but I am not. I am another woman. I don't know where Milly Baines is; perhaps she is in my time and we have got changed somehow, or perhaps I am just dreaming and I cannot wake up. But I do not belong here, I tell you, all my life is in the future, my child, the man I love. You are a man of God. What has happened to me is against God and you must make it right."

Mr. Endworthy said sadly, "How can I do that?"

Melanie said, "By prayer."

Mr. Endworthy waited silently a moment, then made up his mind and sat down. "You are in a nightmare, my poor child," he said, "and what my prayers can do for you, that you shall have. But I want you to look at these dreams of yours with courage and resolution. What has happened to you during these long months I do not ask, although many times I have entreated my Maker that you or your sister should see fit to tell me, and so ease your consciences of the heavy burdens they must bear." He ended on an interrogative note, waiting as if for Melanie to give an explanation, and she cried, "I do not understand you. I have nothing on my conscience. I only want to go home."

Very solemnly Mr. Endworthy said, "But you are going home, my child. And what it may be given me to do to ease your passage, that, with God's help, I shall do."

Melanie cried in terror, "You think I am speaking of death, Mr. Endworthy. I am not. I am speaking of life, real life, where I live and am happy. It is you who are dead, you and Miss Adelaide and this Milly Baines. I am the only one who is alive."

Mr. Endworthy slightly shook his head in hopeless contradiction. Then his tone and expression changed. He said with great earnestness, "Miss Milly, I think that you believe what you are saying to me. You feel that we have all suddenly become strange to you, are all in the past behind you, and that you are on the threshold of a glorious future."

Melanie stared at him in frowning doubt. He had expressed, not her belief, but something approximating to it, a statement that might prove a bridge between their misunderstandings. "It is not quite like that," she began, uncertain whether to step onto the bridge he had built or continue to insist upon what she knew to be true.

"But your belief is correct," said Mr. Endworthy strongly. "It is you who shall enter first into the everlasting life while our still earthbound souls can but envy you your blessed release. You must not be confused or dismayed, dear Milly, if I may in this solemn moment so call you. Almighty God prepares for each of us what future he will, and if, to ease your earthly pain, the promises He holds out to you seem now but of simple earthly pleasure, you must trust that in His infinite goodness He will reveal in good time that truer heavenly bliss for which we all hope and pray."

"I am not going to die," said Melanie desperately. Then a terrible thought entered her mind. She gasped, barely finding enough breath for the words. "Mr. Endworthy, you do not think that this Milly must die before I can go back? No, I can't, I can't. I must go back now, I must. I am — I am too lonely — " and her words died away as she lay with her head falling sideways on the pillow, nothing in her mind but loneliness and terror.

Then she felt Mr. Endworthy's hand on her shoulder. "Listen to me, my dear," he commanded, and again, "Listen now," and with shuddering sighs Melanie composed herself, and at last looked at him again.

He asked, watching her closely, "This future life you see — does it seem to you very real?"

"It *is* real," said Melanie fiercely. "It is the only thing that is real. It is where I belong. I have a husband and a child and I am safe and happy. This is the only thing that is unreal, this nightmare I am in now."

"You believe," he said, "that your soul lives in a future life, and has come back here?"

"Not back," said Melanie. "I have never been here before."

"But someone has been here," he said patiently.

"Whom have I known these many years, if not you?"

"You've known Milly Baines," said Melanie eagerly. Was he beginning to understand? "I don't know what's become of Milly Baines," she said, and then, "Or was I once Milly Baines?" She stared at him, seeking for the answer she was suddenly sure he must know, and he gravely answered her. "I think you were," he said.

"But if I was," said Melanie, painfully thinking, "if I was Milly Baines in the past — "

"You speak of the past, my dear," Mr. Endworthy interrupted, "but it is in the present that we are speaking together, you know."

Melanie demanded of him, "You are sure this is the present? You are quite sure it is real?" and Mr. Endworthy smiled faintly and said, "Quite sure."

"If you are real and this is really happening," said Melanie, "then this is really the past and it can't be changed. Then all this conversation must have happened before, exactly the same, that poor girl not knowing how to get back, perhaps it's often happened — "

"You are not in the future now," said Mr. Endworthy firmly. Perhaps he meant only to recall her from her distressing speculations, but she took it that he was trying to help her search, and asked, "You mean that it can happen only once, that though the past was behind me when I was at home, now the future is in front of me?" And, not waiting for him to reply, she went on, "Then when I was at home, happy, this poor Milly Baines had already had this terrible afternoon, lying here dizzy and trying to explain and no one believing her — " She looked hopefully at Mr. Endworthy, convinced that he was with her in understanding, and that they two together would soon reach the solution, and after the solution, the release.

"This must stop," said Mr. Endworthy, not to her, not to himself, perhaps to God? He stood up again, not now as if on the point of departure, but to embody authority as he looked down on her. "I do not presume," he said, "to understand the ways of my Maker. I can but submit to the doctrines of our Church which has never subscribed to those Eastern beliefs in which the departed soul may return to a new human habitation. Our Church has always set her face firmly against all manner of soothsaying and prophecy, against all those who profess to be able to lift that curtain in which the future is so inscrutably, and, if I may say so, so mercifully veiled. I know that you in some manner believe what you are telling me, and, but for one thing, I might myself have been prepared to believe that, at this dreadful time, our Lord in His infinite mercy had seen fit, not to reveal to you a true future, but to console your pa— " he broke off, and she watched him searching for another phrase with which to continue, "to console you with pleasing visions of those natural pleasures of which your short life has been deprived. But — " he stretched out over the couch a minatory arm, "I cannot so believe. I cannot believe that it is from our Heavenly Father that you have received these dreams that so torment you." His voice grew stronger and denunciatory. "They are from the Devil, these dreams of yours, dreadful payment for sins I know not of, and it is by repentance, only by repentance, that from these terrors you may be freed."

Melanie whimpered, "I will repent, I will repent of anything Milly did, I swear I will repent for her, if you will only pray and release me."

Slowly his arm came down to his side. "You will repent of your sins?" he demanded, and Melanie said weakly, "I will repent," and to her mind she cried, Mine and Milly's, all sins known and unknown I will repent, if only he will pray.

"Do you wish to make a special confession of your sins?" asked Mr. Endworthy, still in the stern voice of priestly authority.

Melanie said fearfully, "Not yet." She had intended to say "Not now" but the words came differently.

"Then let us pray," said Mr. Endworthy, suddenly once more soft and consoling. Tidily and cautiously he arranged himself on his knees beside the couch, and buried his face in his hands.

"O Father of mercies and God of all comfort," prayed Mr. Endworthy, "our only help — " and

Melanie closed her eyes and laid her hands together, fingers to fingers, devoting her whole being to submission and repentance, hearing not the Vicar's words but the sound of his words, trying to drown utterly in submission to divine omnipotence, knowing the waiting and wondering, the waiting and wondering for it to happen, hearing Mr. Endworthy conclude, " — through the merits and mediation of Jesus Christ, thine only Son, our Lord and Saviour. Amen," hearing him shuffle up from his knees, and knowing that to keep her eyes shut or to open them again was equally useless.

Time had been blotted out while he listened to the lark. That was what her mind said in the desolation, and in the instant while the Vicar stood waiting, she had recalled the story that ended with those words, the monk wandering out into the cloister garden to hear the lark, and returning to find that a hundred years had gone by. And I was perceiving the spring, she remembered. I was in ecstasy as I fell asleep, ecstasy one experiences perhaps once, twice, half a dozen times, when to be human is no longer a lonely terror but a glory, when time is blotted out by perfection. Ecstasy is timeless. Is that perhaps the clue? she said; is ecstasy existence in all time and none, and the return into time a random chance, one moment in time's duration as likely as another?

But prayer should be ecstasy, she thought, religious

ecstasy, and she answered herself that this time she had failed to achieve ecstasy through religion, that the simulacrum of ecstasy she was trying to achieve while the Vicar prayed, a total withdrawal into timeless selflessness, the transfiguration of the burden of self into its apotheosis, all this, though sincerely sought, had been feigned. So when prayer works the magic in the books, it is not the words of the prayer, it is not even the prayer, but the ecstasy that is the instrument — it must be the ecstasy, for if it is the prayer or the words of the prayer, then I have tried that magic and it would not restore the pattern, a useless magic, a magic that failed.

I always suspected ecstasy, she said. I knew that it was evil, I said so to Guy — well, not quite so surely as that, but I wondered, I asked him. It was the first time we slept together — no, not the first time, that was all wrong, she admitted, but the second time, remembering the shabby four-poster bed in the hotel in the Forest of Dean. And afterwards, it was like coming back to life from death, and I said to Guy, It can't be right, we can't be meant to endure such bliss, and he was nearly asleep, and he laughed and said I was a puritan at heart. And I asked him if religious people said it was all right to feel ecstasy through God, and he said yes, that was the only kind they thought was right. Then he went to sleep, and outside it was a grey rainy dawn, and I remembered that time when I was sixteen and I was walking alone down South Audley Street and I went into the chapel. There was no one else there and the organ was playing. I sat down and my mind became flooded with God, ecstatic with God, and that time, too, coming back was like coming back to life, exactly the same as when I lay with Guy, the ecstasy identical, whether from man or from God.

It is the ecstasy that is to be feared, she said with shuddering assurance, it is a separation and a severance from reality and time, and it is not safe. The only thing that is safe is to feel only a little, hold tight to time, and never let anything sweep you away as I have been swept — and perhaps that is how, only how I can be swept back.

She had not heard the steps coming up to the front door, but she heard the fall of the knocker, and the bell clanging down in the basement. "That will be Mr. Charters," said the Vicar. He had risen clumsily from his knees and was smiling down at her benignly. "I told him to call for us here." Lizzie's feet were thumping up the stone stairs, the Vicar was turning to the door. With desperate strength Melanie caught at his coat and held him. "I can prove it to you," she cried. "Only wait and listen to me, I can tell you what will happen in the future, machines and horseless carriages and wonderful materials — " If only the words would come out right, the words that should say refrigerator and plastics and atom bomb — "If you will only listen, I can prove it to you," she entreated, for if only he would understand and believe, then, surely then, the prayer would be efficacious. But he only said absently, not even turning to look at her, "You've been reading Old Mother Shipton, I see," and with an expectant smile he cocked his head towards the door, listening to Lizzie's footsteps along the hall that were joined by Adelaide's, coming — now Melanie strained to listen too — coming not from up or down the stairs but from the bedroom behind the communicating-doors.

Now Mr. Endworthy did turn to Melanie to say with quick reassurance, "This house is very stoutly built. I do not think that anything could have been overheard," and then, seemingly caught by the despair on her face, he said to her with sincere kindness, "There is nothing to be afraid of, Miss Milly."

These words, thought Melanie, are meant. Now he is speaking not as Mr. Endworthy the Victorian clergyman but out of timelessness. He is telling me that it will be all right and that I shall go home again. So in relief almost beyond bearing she smiled at him and loosened her frenzied grip on his coat, and he smiled back and said playfully, "Miss Milly, you are still a very pretty little girl when you smile." They had both heard, through this interchange, the voices in the hall, Lizzie's and Adelaide's and the strong young voice of Mr. Charters — a voice at whose sound Melanie's heart suddenly leapt, and then recovered itself, leaving her wondering. "All right now?" said Mr. Endworthy quickly to Melanie, and they were both smiling when the door opened, and Adelaide came in with Mr. Charters behind her.

Melanie noticed with surprise that Adelaide was differently dressed now, with some sort of cloak or mantle over her shoulders and a wide black bonnet lined with white set on her looped dark hair. And then she looked behind Adelaide and she saw Mr. Charters, and a shiver, a strange desirous urgent shiver ran through her body, and everything was changed because she had seen Mr. Charters again.

He must at least touch my hand, she said avidly to herself, he cannot help but touch my hand, and she gazed at him, willing him to come nearer and touch her. But it was only for a second that he allowed his eyes to meet hers. "Good afternoon, Miss Milly," he said and bowed, but he looked away from her as soon as he had started to speak, and hurriedly continued, turning to the Vicar, "I do trust that I am not late, sir. I was detained by old Graves."

The Vicar pulled a gold half-hunter from an inner pocket. "You are only five minutes past the appointed time," he said jovially, "and Miss Milly and I have made good use of those five minutes."

Why did both Adelaide and Mr. Charters start slightly as he spoke, start, and then look round quickly as if to be sure that no one else had noticed, not even the other? "Do you know if Miss Rampole will be coming?" the Vicar asked, and while Adelaide and

Mr. Charters offered information and surmises in reply, Melanie gazed on Mr. Charters, demanding that her mind or Milly's should tell her why he should affect her with such powerful longing and pain.

I have never seen him before, Melanie told herself, looking at the light brown curly hair and beard, the ruddy complexion, the soft sweet mouth. I am sure I have never seen him before, and I want him more than any man I have ever met — no, she said, remembering, not more than Guy. I want him as I used to want Guy that wicked week in Gloucestershire before we were married, when every time I looked at him in the daytime, in the hotel dining room with other people there, anywhere at all, I used to remember his hands on me, his mouth on mine, and I shivered with wanting that he should touch me, kiss me, take me again. Gilbert, come to me again, cried a voice through her mind, and Melanie demanded of herself, What did I say, what name did I say? I cannot want him like this if it is the first time I've met him, she cried, while around her the pretty social chat went on; if I feel to him as I did to Guy and to no other man, perhaps he is Guy. Perhaps he is Guy, she repeated, Guy in the past or Guy in my dream, perhaps we have been together before, or perhaps, because we love each other so much, even in our dreams we are together. But if he is Guy, why won't he look at me, why is he so careful not to look at me, so frightened of looking at me? Could Guy look, have looked like that? she wondered, the same colour hair, Guy's mouth isn't soft like that, but if he'd been the only son of a widow, spoilt and petted, it might have been like that. I don't think he's Guy, but I can't be sure. How can I feel like this to a stranger when I have felt like this only to Guy?

Now she heard their conversation again. "What news do you have of Miss Tufnell?" Adelaide was asking Mr. Charters with something new in her voice, a kind of arch playfulness. The Vicar, too, was smiling, and only Mr. Charters seemed uncomfortable, even embarrassed, as he answered, "She has been up in Darjeeling with her mamma, visiting acquaintances there." He half turned, as if he could not help it, to shoot an apprehensive glance at Melanie, then turned back as he continued, "She writes that the Colonel was detained in Bengal on regimental business."

"It is in September that she returns, is it not?" asked Adelaide, still smiling, and the Vicar answered for Mr. Charters, "And in October the wedding bells will ring, and then both my curates will have pretty little wives to comfort them in their tribulations."

Not October, cried Melanie to herself, not so soon, no, it cannot happen, something will surely prevent it. She must have spoken aloud, at least the first words, for the Vicar turned and said, "You think a spring wedding is prettier, Miss Milly? I must confess that I agree with you, but after so long, our good friend is naturally anxious to set up his establishment. How long is it since you have seen your intended bride, Gilbert?" he asked, and Mr. Charters answered, "In September it will be just over three years," and again he shot that strange quick glance at Melanie.

The Vicar had been holding his watch in his hand. "I think we should be on our way now," he said, and Adelaide came to the couch and said with faint worry, "You are sure you are still feeling fit to be left, Milly? The bell is by your hand and — wait — I had better leave some syrup of laudanum in case you cough — " She went to a small carved cupboard in the corner and, while she busied herself with bottle and glass, Mr. Charters, still not looking directly at Melanie, said awkwardly, "I hope your cough has not been too troublesome of late, Miss Milly."

I must fight, said Melanie to herself, I must be well and able to fight, not a poor weak thing tied to a sofa. She smiled at him, deliberately remembering how she had smiled at Guy, and it was in the voice that she had answered Guy's solicitous questions that she replied, "It troubles me less and less, Mr. Charters, but it is kind, no, more than kind of you to enquire." Mr. Endworthy must have heard something new in her voice, for he turned quickly and said with surprise, "Why, that is the best news I have heard today, Miss Milly," and then Adelaide was back beside the couch with a sticky brown liquid in a small thick glass, and over it a little muslin cover weighted with blue beads.

"I think that is all," she said. She bent and laid her mittened hand on Melanie's forehead, then withdrew it, apparently satisfied. "I am ready," she said to the gentlemen, and Mr. Endworthy passed by the couch on his way to the door, pausing to say, "Good night, Miss Milly. God bless you," and then behind him, coming towards the couch, was Mr. Charters, looking quickly at the backs of Adelaide and the Vicar and then quickly, furtively, moving his hand towards Milly.

He is going to touch me, she said, trembling, despite everything he could not go without touching me — and then, at the door, Adelaide turned, and in that instant, as if it had never moved, Mr. Charter's hand was back at his side again.

"I had forgotten about the doctor," Adelaide said in a vexed tone, explaining to Mr. Endworthy, "We sent for him earlier, when Milly seemed rather poorly. I wonder if, after all, I had better wait in case he comes."

"Do you think he will come as late as this?" Mr. Endworthy suggested, but Adelaide said, "He is very devoted. Of course I could send Lizzie — but I do not like to leave my sister alone."

"But we can walk round that way," said Mr. Endworthy, with the satisfaction of one who finds the solution. "It will take us only a very few minutes longer, and since it results from Miss Milly feeling better, it is time well spent."

"How very kind of you," said Adelaide with obvious relief, "I must confess I should have been sorry to miss — " and Melanie lost the last words as Adelaide passed through the door and was followed by the gentlemen into the hall.

The door was not tightly shut behind them, and Melanie could hear that Mr. Endworthy was putting on his galoshes, his coat, his hat. Then she heard Mr. Charters exclaim, "My gloves — no, don't trouble — " and he pushed open the door and came back into the room.

For an instant he stood beside the couch, gazing down at her with infinite misery and pain. Then he was on his knees beside her, his face against hers. "Melly!" — or so it seemed to her — "Melly!" he groaned, and then quickly rose to his feet and was gone.

And soon they were all gone, the front door closed decisively behind them, and Melanie left alone. He had to come back, she was telling herself delightedly, it is not all over, in the end he will still come back to me — and then, in appalled realisation, she said aloud, "To me?" and next, still speaking aloud but now in soft horror, "When he was there, I was not me. I was Milly Baines."

Fear was like seasickness, it came in great waves, a thunderous beat that drummed in the stomach and made the whole body vibrate. But who was afraid, Milly or Melanie, Milly lost to Melanie or Melanie lost to Milly or both into one? I spoke as Milly when I told her Mr. Endworthy was here, she remembered, and then, But he called Melly. I heard him call me Melly. Somehow he is linked with my being Melanie — and, clinging to that thought, I am Melanie, not Milly. I am there, not here, that is real, not this, and at last the sick shuddering anguish again died down.

But this time it left a new conscious fear behind, the fear of Melanie again being overwhelmed by Milly, that the moments when Melanie could be only, surely Melanie would grow shorter and shorter, as seasickness will come back again and again, as the lucid intervals between fevers are weighted with the certainty that the fever will return. I must think while there's time, cried Melanie. I must find the pattern, a new pattern, the right pattern.

He called me Melly, she repeated, and if he did, then he and this feeling I had for him, are they somehow linked with the pattern? For an instant she felt his body on hers, and beneath her the hard patterning of the embroidered felt of the chaise longue, and then enormous disgust blotted the picture out. He is dead, thought Melanie, to link love and death is horrible, to think of being touched by the dead. Only Guy can touch me and love me; I must find the pattern and get back to Guy. Don't think of death, she told herself, not of love or of making love, not of Gilbert or of Guy, only of the problem that is made

up of pieces shaken at random, yet able to be re-
formed into the pattern of truth and reality.

Is it perhaps a challenge? she wondered. Tentatively she examined the suggestion; did challenge con-
tain the necessary formulation of pattern? Did someone — Fate, Providence, God? — place me here to
see how I did, and if I do right, then I shall be free?
That is a pattern, she decided excitedly, now I have
only to settle what is right — and this was not difficult, for the phrases forged by the many, many gen-
erations needing courage were waiting in the store-
house of her mind. To master my fate, to smile in
the face of danger, to keep my head, grasp the nettle,
put a bold face on it, go out to meet it, struggle and
strive and do the best one can. No other answer had
the hammered tested weight of this one. Not to wait
passively, then, thought Melanie, accepting the answer, to strive and fight and do the best I can, and
someone, watching, will assess and judge, award the
marks, decide if I pass or fail. And I shall pass, she
said strongly, and the first thing I need is to be well,
to conquer this weakness that leaves me lying here,
which is not my weakness, but Milly Baines's. I,
Melanie, can be strong and well.

Slowly she pressed her elbows into the couch,
raised her right arm until her hand caught and held
the scrolled wooden carving that topped its curved
back piece. Of course it will be difficult at first, she

told herself reassuringly, because I have not tried; I've accepted this weakness that was Milly's, but now of my own strength I shall overcome it. Waiting, postponing the test, she asked herself, And then if I pass this one? If I can sit up and smile and laugh, what must I do with it? How many tests before it lets me through?

And again the traditional phrases supplied the answer — the job that lies to hand, the station of life to which it shall please, uncomplainingly to take up the heavy burden. So, she translated, I must succeed as Milly, be a brave, good Milly, repent as Milly — the last phrase she did not choose and wondered at. I will do all that, she promised, but not, please, not for too long. I cannot lie down to sleep as Milly, alone in the dark smelly night, awake as Milly to another horrible day; but as she expressed these last fears she knew somehow that they were no more real than the fear of the train crash or the ship sinking or the lightning striking. She was nearly sure that she would not lie down to sleep as Milly, lie alone as Milly in the dark, and as Milly wake up again to another day.

Now, she said, now is long enough, if I wait longer I shall have failed, and she dug her elbows into the couch and clung with her hand to the wooden scrolling. Her hand was so weak it could hardly hold, her head was so dazed she could hardly lift it. Let go, screamed the muscles in the arm, let me sink, let me rest, screamed the shaking brain, but Melanie clung with the hand and lifted the head, dug in with the elbows, and, pushing and pulling and struggling, inch by inch shifted the aching thighs and buttocks, and at last she was sitting, still clinging, still holding on, her back against the curved headrest of the chaise longue.

Will that do? she asked in triumph, but there was no answer. I didn't really expect it would be enough, she told herself quickly, there is still being the good brave Milly, kind to Adelaide, noble, making up for everything. First I must wait for my head to stop rocking inside, and then I will raise it again and sit upright. If I sit upright, I shall be active, not quiescent. I shall master this world.

She waited, but still her head dizzied and swung and swirled. At last it was impossible not to say that she had waited long enough. Her right hand was numb with the effort of holding, but still she clung, and then she lifted her head from the headrest and raised her spine. She was sitting upright, she was leaning forward, bent over the taut tired arm and coughing and coughing and coughing.

And as she crouched there, bent over her outstretched right arm, unable to stop the painful torturing cough, her left hand, will-less, was fumbling among the coverings, fumbling and searching and then finding, raising itself to her contorted mouth, pressing against it the horrible soft familiarity, and still the coughing went on and the body slipped back on the sofa, the exhausted arm slipped and fell back on the coverlet, and Melanie was lying back again, crumpled and done, the cough at last subsiding, and her eyes watching her left hand bring away from her mouth the bloodstained handkerchief.

So Milly has T.B. too, she whispered, but she whispered it aloud, and what she said was "Milly has the consumption." Milly and I, both consumptive — but I am not consumptive, she remembered sharply, I am nearly well, I am cured. She looked at the handkerchief, shining wet with bright red blood. I never coughed blood, she said in horror, you only cough blood if you're — if you're nearly — but this time it was simply fear that would not let the words be said. And nobody ever got cured in those days, she thought, down into the grave, the beautiful, the strong. I could be cured, but not they. And how, she cried, can I pass the test if Milly's decaying body will not let me do it?

So that pattern would not do. That was not the shape of the ordeal, to be Melanie in Milly, brave Melanie replacing tired dejected Milly. Suddenly she thought, Then it is to save her, to save her life, that is why I have been sent back here, because I know how to save Milly, fresh air and sunlight and milk and rest — but then, with equal suddenness, the question, Save whom? Save Milly, or save me? I in this body, I in Milly's dying body, must I die in Milly's body because it is too soon to be saved? But I know how to be saved, she said, surely this is the test and the ordeal, to save Milly and myself, to save and be saved?

But the cough was coming again, the terrifying destructive cough. The syrup, it should be there, she thought, and remembered, Yes, Adelaide left it there. She fumbled on the table, twitching the muslin cover off the glass, clumsily sliding the glass from the table, the tatted cover pulled all awry, but before she could raise the glass to her lips the cough was upon her again, her chin on her breast, chin and breast jerking convulsively together and the glass leaping and jerking in her hand.

This time she did not hear the feet on the steps outside, the knocking and ringing, the feet in the passage, or was it, she wondered, in the second of time it took the door to open, unnecessary that the feet should mount the steps or the hand pull the bell, since in dreams they could come and go senselessly and without causation, no world outside with cause and effect stretching to the ends of the universe? "The doctor, miss," said Lizzie's coarse voice, and as Melanie coughed in helpless pain and waited for him to come to her, she thought, It is him I must convince, not the hard way, not the way it really happened, but somehow to show him how I can be cured.

She could not look yet because her eyes were closed with the coughing, but she felt his chilly hand brush her neck as he passed his arm behind her shoulders and lifted her a little, so that at last the intolerable pressure was eased and the cough subsided into dry choking gasps. He had taken the glass from her hand and was holding it against her lips, and she lapped at it avidly, needing the stupefaction of pain this glutinous syrup could bring. Then she looked at him and she thought, This is not a good doctor. Mr. Endworthy was a good clergyman, but this man will not do. And I have never seen him before — this with relief she was sure of, looking at the lank black hair, the pale dull face, the drooping black moustaches. "I am sorry to find you so distressed," he said listlessly, and she knew that he had expected nothing else because he had long since decided how this case was going, and it was beyond his skill to alter it.

But that's not fair to me, she felt angrily, if the doctor isn't intelligent, then the odds are too heavy and there's nothing I can do. Then she thought, Perhaps it's not that he is stupid, only hopeless, and if I can convince him with strength and good sense, he will change. He was feeling her pulse now and looking at a big silver turnip watch he held in his hand, not a gold watch like Mr. Endworthy's, but the silver watch of the not too successful doctor.

How shall I phrase it, Melanie asked herself, not to make him dismiss it instantly, thinking only that I am delirious or mad? Cautiously groping after each word, she decided upon, "Do you trust in instinct?" and opened her mouth to say it, but the words would not come.

"Here," said the doctor, looking at her gaping mouth, and he picked up the barley water and held it out to her. Melanie shook her head, and he waited patiently, seeming unsurprised that the words should take so long to come.

Why cannot I say *that?* Melanie asked herself in surprise. I know now that I can't talk here of things that didn't exist, but instinct existed, the word and the thing. Why can't I say it? — and then an answer suggested itself, that the word could not be said because Milly Baines did not know it, poor silly Milly Baines with her weakened wits that were more powerful than Melanie's. But I was never clever, she reflected, I know only what ordinary people know, just like Milly does, but in the future — but *now*, she corrected herself in terror, ordinary people know so much more. I know I'm silly compared with clever people, but Milly is silly compared with me. "Milly is silly," she said aloud, and to her surprise she said it smiling and met an answering smile of complicity on the doctor's face, as if it were a joke that had been made many times before.

"Milly is *very* silly," the doctor answered with mock severity, and lightly pinched her cheek. "But Milly's going to be a good girl now, isn't she?" He looked less dull, less stupid when he smiled, though the smile was a fond and foolish one. He was disgusted by me before, Melanie discovered, he has some other picture of me than lying decaying here. Then was it he — ? she asked herself, and then, He who — what? What has any man to do with this, except Guy, who is waiting for me?

She did not choose the coy playful voice in which she asked, "Is Philip going to help me to be a good girl?" and she was not surprised when he replied archly, "Milly knows how to be a bad girl without any help from Philip, doesn't she?" He was suddenly angry as he finished, and he grasped her shoulders tightly, hurting her as he demanded, "Why didn't Milly ask Philip's help if she wanted to be naughty?"

Melanie gasped, "You're hurting me," but the doctor's fingers only dug more tightly into her shoulders and his head came down threateningly close to hers. "I want to hurt you," he said savagely, "You like to be hurt, don't you? You don't always scream and flutter and protest when a man hurts you. Oh God, if I had known — "

"You're hurting me," Melanie repeated, her voice lifting in surprise, and then he released her and straightened himself. Looking down at her, he said with tired anger, "You thought I was a fool, didn't you, you and that sister of yours. *Oh, Milly's so much better, she really needs no medical attention. I fear it would only worry her to see the doctor.*" He spoke in a high, artificial treble, and Melanie realised that, without attempting any likeness other than that of a general corrupt femininity, it was Adelaide's voice he was mimicking. "For six months," he said in his own angry voice, "I didn't see you, no one saw you, just the same story — " the mimicry came again, *"Oh yes, doctor, she's doing very nicely, stronger every day, you did her so much good with your treatment — "* He broke off and said with hatred, "But it wasn't *my* treatment that did you good, was it, Milly?"

"You shouldn't talk like this," cried Melanie fiercely, meaning that no doctor should talk like this, destroying and not helping, blaming her for some uncomprehended ill-doing of Milly Baines. "You are a doctor," she said, reproaching him, and he echoed, "Yes, I am a doctor. That's what you both forgot when you called me in again — " Again he quoted, the mimicry a ridiculous quack-quack. *"Oh, Dr. Blundell, my poor sister, she's had a relapse. Oh, Dr. Blundell, do come and see her again."*

"I am sure Adelaide never spoke like that," said Melanie, untouched by him, wanting only to restore him to detached doctorhood so that he could listen and help.

"Something like that," he said roughly, refusing to be diverted from his rage. "I tell you, I'm a doctor," he repeated. "Did you really think, you fools, that as soon as I saw you again I shouldn't instantly know?" His face changed, the angry lines smoothed then re-shaped into drooping lines of pain. Tears came into his eyes. "Oh, Milly," he cried, "why didn't you tell me? Why wouldn't you trust me? Didn't you know I would help you?"

I can use this mood, said Melanie coldly to herself. She smiled at him as she had smiled at Gilbert Charters, as she used to smile at Guy, but knowing that the smile did not speak, as she had thought when she gave it to Guy, of desires permissible and pure, but of darker, disastrous knowledge. "Why did you not tell me before that you would help me?" she asked.

"Could I?" he demanded, tears in his voice. "When have I had the opportunity? Every time she has been here, watching you, watching me, never even turning her back to allow me a private glance. Only this evening, when her message came, I knew it was my chance at last. I could pretend I had not received it and see you alone. And God knows why I have come."

"You have come to help me," said Melanie softly, looking up at him from under her eyelashes.

"It is too late," he cried, and he sank on his knees beside the chaise longue, his arm across her body. "Milly, why did you not tell me before? I would have done anything, right or wrong, but now there is nothing I can do."

What is the fool weeping about? thought Melanie with a new impatient cruelty, she who was soft and kind as she had thought — could she have been wrong? — that Milly was soft and kind too. She put out a hand and touched his neck, shuddering as she touched it, but forcing her fingers to stroke and caress. "Forget the past," she whispered. "You can help me now if only you will."

"But I cannot," he cried, and he dropped his face on to her breast and sobbed.

"Philip," said Melanie softly, and then, more sharply, "Philip!" He raised his head and looked at her, and she said — knowing that for the moment she had conquered him and the authority was hers — "Philip, I beg of you, sit down and let me speak to you. There is so little time, and you are the only one who can help." Despite herself, her voice broke as she begged, "Philip, please let me speak to you in calmness, I implore you."

Clumsily he climbed to his feet and looked at her with a half-distrust. "You are sincere?" he asked. "You are not seeking, even now, to make a fool of me again?"

"I swear I am sincere," said Melanie, and then quickly, "Take Adelaide's chair, Philip, and come and sit beside me. If you will help me, if I can lean on your strength, I know that all will be well."

For a moment he still looked at her doubtfully, then went and fetched the chair as she had asked, and placed it by the chaise longue. But when he had seated himself and was waiting for her to begin, his face had regained the sullen dullness with which he had first greeted her, and the task of rousing him to the belief that could help seemed again impossible. It was because of this that she began, not cautiously, as she had intended, but shockingly. "You believe I am going to die."

But he was not, as she had expected, shocked into vehement denial. Instead he nodded his head and agreed, "Yes, you are going to die. Nobody and nothing can do anything to save you now."

It was Melanie who was outraged. Doctors did not say such things. Forgetting her deliberate plan she burst out, "You don't really think so, do you?"

He said impatiently, "Milly, for God's sake, what are you trying to make me say? Do you want me to pretend? I thought we were to be honest at last."

"Of course," she said quickly, telling herself that what he thought didn't matter, Milly's living or dying being unreal, a story, and the need to save her nothing but the instrument of release for Melanie, nothing in terms of real living and dying. Carefully now, back to the plan, she asked, "Do you think it reasonable, Philip, that creatures like ourselves should feel strongly what is good for them, what they need, even if their minds cannot explain it?"

The doctor was looking at her differently now. "That is a strange question for you to ask, Milly," he said. "I did not know that you thought about such things."

"I have been forced to think about such things,"

said Melanie gravely. "Philip, please answer my question."

The sullen languor was gone now, his interest as lively as when he had attacked her, but this time impersonal, directed solely to her question.

"I think it reasonable to suppose that human beings may sometimes have some such faculty as you suggest," he answered, "that is to say that they may have such a faculty in a condition of natural savagery where its exercise may be necessary for survival, just as a horse, by his natural sagacity, will refuse to drink tainted water, or a mouse that has never before seen a cat still knows it to be an enemy. But I doubt whether such a faculty survives in civilised beings. Certainly they have desires," he laughed shortly, "but their desires are more often self-destructive than curative."

"And yet one can tell," Melanie suggested, "one knows in one's heart whether such desires are good or bad."

"Did you know?" he asked, retaining his detached tone, but adding to it contempt and cruelty. "Or did you perhaps satisfy your desires because nature told you it would be good for you to do so?"

"Philip, forget the past," said Melanie wearily. It seemed to be necessary to say this. "I am speaking of the present, of the future."

"You have no future," he said.

Melanie cried, "Philip, I know, I know, I tell you,

how I can be saved. Only listen and let me tell you."

"Very well," he said. "Tell me."

She had not meant to speak like this, quickly, excitedly, the words stumbling over each other. "I need fresh air and sunlight," she said. "I need to go somewhere where the air is pure and clean, to the mountains where I can lie in the sun and drink clean milk and grow strong. If you will take me to the mountains I shall recover, I know I shall, and Philip, I will give you everything, everything you ever wanted, if only you will help me."

He sneered, "Do you think that I want you now?"

"Listen to what I say," she cried. "Can't you tell that I'm speaking the truth? I know that I can be cured if I can be in the sunlight, in the fresh air." She was weeping now, sobbing uglily as he himself had sobbed. "I know," she gasped, "I know that would save me. Save me, Philip, don't let me die."

His arms were round her, he was holding her, consoling her, not hating her any more. "Do you think I would let you die if I could save you?" he said, his mouth in her hair, and she cried, "Try, only try. Open the window, that's all I ask, open the window and let me breathe the air, and I shall be better, you will see, I shall be better instantly."

"Milly," he groaned, "dear Milly, stop, I entreat you. How can I do what you wish?" "Why not?" she wept, and he said, "Milly, if I open the window, the cold air will come in, the fog will come in, they will strike at your chest, you will cough and cough, and you know that to cough is the worst thing for you. Your only hope is to keep from currents of air, to keep warm and protected — " "But I know," she screamed, interrupting him, and his pained sad voice answered, "You cannot know, Milly dear, believe me, you cannot know. These are sick fancies arising from your poor tired brain." He let her back gently on the pillow, and stood up, lifting the chair and replacing it by the fireside. His back turned to her, she still caught his softly spoken words, "It is too late for you to know anything at all," and his words seemed to have the force of Mr. Endworthy's promise that there was nothing to fear, to erase Mr. Endworthy's words and cancel them out. "I must go now," he said, coming back to the couch. "I do not want to meet Miss Adelaide this evening." "I will ring for Lizzie," said Milly weakly, knowing what was proper, and he, too, recalled to convention, insisted, "Do not trouble, I beg you — I can show myself out."

He looked at her and she at him. There was nothing more they had to say to each other. He bowed to her and went.

She heard his footsteps in the hall, the door opening and closing again, and sighed because these noises meant reality, because their absence would have meant the certain proof of nightmare. "It is time for the lamps," she said aloud. "What can the girl be thinking of?" and it was indeed growing dark behind the dusty lace curtains, the dirty yellow daylight changed to a dark green-grey. "As soon as Adelaide is not here — " she began, and then stopped as she heard the expected heavy steps on the stone stairs.

And Lizzie came in with the lamp already lit, a sturdy brass lamp with a frilled pink shade. She set it down on the table in the window, and drew the curtains, but clumsily, so that the right-hand one was caught up against one of the chairs. "Lizzie, the curtain," said Milly sharply, and Lizzie looked and said, "Beg pardon, miss," and twitched it straight. She came to the fireplace and lit the gas brackets with the expected pop and then paused by the chaise longue to say, "Is there anything I could get you, miss, before Miss Adelaide gets back?"

At last, thought Milly, and she said urgently, "Quickly, Lizzie, could you — ?" and Lizzie broke in, "Not this time, miss. I daren't do it. She'll be back any minute now, you know she will, and anyway she'd smell it like she did last time." She paused at the door to repeat, "I daren't do it, miss," and as the door closed behind her, Milly picked up the glass of laudanum and drained its last dregs, but they were not enough, not enough to still the hunger.

"Why, I want a drink!" said Melanie aloud, and then angrily, No harm in that, is there? Such a little comfort, such a little comfort to ask for. "Of course there's no harm," said Melanie to Milly. "We often have a drink, there's no harm whatsoever, only people saying there is." I want it now, I want it now, she moaned, I started because he said it would save me, it didn't work though he said it would, but I got used to it and it helped and made me forget. "It's wrong to *need* it," said Melanie, and then, But I can't help it, it's not I that need it but this body, we need it to forget, so much to forget, all the future and all the past.

We seem to be together now, she explained, you and I both hopeless. I think we did the same things, she told her, we loved a man and we flirted and we took little drinks, but when I did those things there was nothing wrong, and for you it was terrible punishable sin. It was no sin for Melanie, she explained carefully, because the customs were different; sin changes, you know, like fashion. There can be no punishment for Melanie, only for you, and now the other side of the conversation awoke, the answer came, saying, But how do I know this is punishment, I was ill before it happened, would I be well if I were sinless? It was warm with the lamp and the gas jets, and the body on the chaise longue was drowsy and bathed in sweat. Everything has been tried, murmured Melanie, and the pattern did not appear. It is easiest to give up, to live here and die here because there is nothing more to try.

The right-hand gas jet spluttered and burned blue for a moment and then recovered itself. Melanie shook herself awake with a shudder. She nearly caught me, she said, her eyes wide open, and then, I will not give up. There must be something still to try.

"Melly," he had said, calling her by the name only Guy had called her — I am nearly sure, she told herself, that he said Melly, not Milly, then, quickly, Yes, I am sure, I am quite sure. Of course that was the pattern, the only link — there, if she could discover it, the pattern must lie hidden. I knew him, I knew his body, she remembered excitedly. Have we been together, or is it still to come? I remember his body on mine on the chaise longue. I remembered that when I first saw the chaise longue, and I remembered it again here. I thought of ecstasy, she said excitedly, ecstasy brought me here, ecstasy will take me back. Gilbert, come, she shouted silently, come, come, straining towards him, willing him to come to her, to take her on the chaise longue and so release her.

And then again, at the thought of it, came the horror, the disgust that there should be linked, even in thought, the living body and the dead. I am alive and he is dead, she said, and then slowly, for the first time, she asked herself, Whose body is this that I am in? Is this my living body, my, Melanie's, living body? Can a mind be in a strange body, or is it my body that is here, rotting and dying? No, if it is my body, then it is a dream, a delusion, she cried. The body can live only once, and the mind lives and feeds on the body. If this is my body, then I am safe. I have only to wait and the illusion that clouds my mind must pass. However long it seems, an instant or a lifetime, I must be freed, because my body, I know with absolute certainty, is there and there no time can have passed, so that the moment will surely come when the sunlight is still in the window and all the softness and sweet smells and love of home. Oh, I want to go home, she moaned. There has never been a loss like this loss, this unimaginable separation from life. Let me go home, she pleaded, I am so homesick, so frightened and lonely, there is no shape or pattern and nothing I can do, and I dare not discover that this body isn't mine.

But even while she cried and moaned, she was holding her hands up before her eyes, and presently her sobs quieted as all her attention became fixed upon her hands. The nails were short and cut clumsily with scissors, and tight cuticles grew over the half-moons. There's nothing to that, Melanie told herself, breathing quickly, naturally if I dream it, I would dream it right, Milly would have nails like this, not pointed nails, pink-painted. I think these are my fingers, she said doubtfully, there was nothing particular to remember about my fingers, they were long and thin, and so are these. I could just span my wrist with my thumb and forefinger, she remembered, and now, trying it, she found that the span was easily made, more easily than she remembered. But Milly has been ill, more ill than I, ill for longer than I, so naturally her wrists would be thinner. I am nearly sure these are my hands, she said, and fear shouted, But you must be sure, sure, sure.

She put up her hands to touch her face, a finger over her lips, her eyebrows, sliding down her nose. I think so, she said, until she felt the hair on her head, but this was strange. She could feel smooth loops down over her ears — of course it would be dressed like Adelaide's. But the colour, she thought, and she pulled a hair from under the left-hand loop and laid it across her palm to examine it.

It was hard to be sure from a single hair. It looks darker than mine — but then mine had had camomile rinses and hot sun shining on it, of course mine would be lighter than Milly's. I must have a looking glass, she thought desperately, and then rejected this in terror. A glass could be too sure, too wrongly sure, corrupted and lying because it came from here, not there. Better to proceed slowly, nearly sure on the side of safety and right, than wrongly sure and lost.

I know my body, she said suddenly, if I know anything in the world I know my body.

I must find my body, she said desperately, and her fingers were scrabbling at the garments she wore, scrabbling uselessly and finding no entry.

Go slowly, she said to herself, go slowly. You cannot undress until you know what you are wearing. Her hands crept over her shoulders, there was something loose over her shoulders; on and on crept the exploring hands, to the neck and a small satin bow. I can undo this, she said, and the ribbons fell down over her hands, narrow mauve satin ribbons that had held closely round her neck a shaped white loosely knitted shawl, falling over her shoulders and the top of her arms in a frilled cape. Now up again from the cotton frills at the wrist, up the sleeves, up to the neck, a frill at the neck, down the front — I can see, she said, it is a white cotton nightgown, thick, heavy white cotton, it fastens down the front with pearl buttons, and I can undo them.

Underneath the nightgown there was flannel, too often washed and hard and felted. This flannel also unfastened down the front, silk featherstitching outlining the placket, and little crumpled white buttons made of thread over a frame like spiders' webs. I can undo those buttons, said Melanie, and she undid them, pushed back the shawl and the nightgown and the vest, and now she could look at her body.

But now she did not dare. Even if it is not my body, it will prove nothing, she said, disbelieving herself, but striving to be convinced. When I was a child and Miss Paine was late in fetching me from school, I used to pray to God, Even if she has not got on the next bus that is coming, I would pray, make it as if she had got onto the next bus, You could do it, change the whole universe so that no one will know and it will seem as if she had always got on the next bus. And if the next bus didn't bring her, I would think that God had denied me, but if the next bus came and Miss Paine got off, then I knew that really she would have been on the bus after that or the one after that, but that God had granted my prayer and changed the universe so that she could come to me more quickly. That could happen, she said, if I could imagine it, then it could happen. It may happen often, all the time, so that there is no continuity of time, but that continuity is the only way we are capable of imagining it. Time may be going not in a straight line but in all directions and in no direction, and God may have changed the universe so that it is my body that lies here and no dream, or not my body and still a dream from which I shall be freed.

The test of courage is still valid, said her conscience, you must know, you must look. So she lifted her head and looked down at her body.

There, framed by the crumpled clothes, set on ribs barely covered with skin, rose two small breasts. My breasts? cried Melanie, or not my breasts? Dare I touch them, these breasts that may be mine and alive, or will they crumble, will they rot if I touch them with my living hands, my hands on long-dead breasts? These are whiter than mine, she said, smaller, sadder than mine, and in a convulsive movement she laid her hands beneath them and they did not rot, small hot living breasts, and, pulsing through them, the too-fast-beating heart.

I think they are mine, she said, my hands fit them

as if they were mine — or as Milly's hands fitted hers? Oh, I should know my body, she cried, but how should I know it? I loved it because it was perfect and unstained, there was no mark or scar by which I should know it. Look closely, look closely, she cried, and there, running down from the breast bone to each nipple, was the new blue swollen vein.

This body has borne a child, my child. Melanie screamed, and outside the door the slow noises quickened into scurrying convulsion. "Where is my baby?" she screamed. "Give me my baby, I want my baby," screaming for her baby as she fell back on the chaise longue, her clothes torn aside and her naked breasts shaking as she screamed.

"You are mad," shouted Adelaide. "You are foul, you are mad." Her hands were among the clothes, pulling them together, covering the revealing fecund breasts.

"What have you done with my baby?" screamed Melanie, reaching up, clutching at Adelaide, clawing at Adelaide's breast as if her clothes, too, should be torn from that arid bosom.

"You promised," panted Adelaide. "You swore you would never ask, never say a word if I kept you and looked after you. You swore," and still Melanie screamed, "Give me my baby, I want my baby."

Adelaide tore herself from the clawing hands, and, crumpled and dishevelled, Melanie dropped back in a helpless untidy heap.

"I want my baby," she moaned, "I want my baby," and Adelaide watched her, breathing heavily as she watched, her eyes glittering.

Suddenly she leant forward, her mouth close to Melanie's head that was twisted sideways on the pillow. "Would you like to see your baby?" she whispered, slowly, cruelly, and then, as Melanie ceased her moaning to listen, "You shall see your baby if you tell me who he was," and, straightening herself, she said, ordering compliance, "Tell me his name and you shall see your baby."

Gasping, trying to control her hysterical sobs, Melanie looked up at her. "I cannot tell you," she said, "for I do not know."

Adelaide smacked her face, with the right hand and with the left. "Slut!" she screamed. "Slut! Filthy slut!" pulling the clothes aside again, beating Melanie on the head, the breast, unable to stop until Melanie's head jerked up and forward and she coughed and then coughed again, and suddenly her mouth was full of hot metallic blood that gushed out, over the punishing hands, over the clothes and the covers and the roses on the chaise longue, and the head fell sideways over the edge and the body twitched and then lay limp.

So Milly is dying, explained the voice in Melanie's brain, knowing that the body had been carried to the bed behind the double doors and that around the bed were Adelaide and Mr. Charters and the doctor, Mr. Charters on his knees, his hands covering the tears that fell, the intensity of his muttered prayers hiding the sobs that shook him. "We humbly commend the soul of this Thy servant, our dear sister — " she heard, and the muttering rose and fell, sometimes words, sometimes a dull hopeless hum, and in silence Adelaide and the doctor stood and watched.

Who is dying? cried the fainting voice, only Milly, it can only be Milly. I am not in that body, sinking and unconscious, we are only waiting for release, Milly to death and I to life. I can see them around me, Adelaide and Mr. Charters and the doctor — "Her eyes are open," whispered Adelaide, and the doctor, "She can see nothing now, rest assured, she can see nothing now" — and beyond them she could see the drawing room over the canal, Dr. Gregory and Sister Smith and Guy, their backs to her, bending over the chaise longue. Was there agony in them as they stood there, terror and certainty of loss, or were they smiling and untroubled and confident of continuance? She could not know, there was no way to tell, but there they stood, Dr. Gregory and Sister Smith and Guy, Adelaide and Mr. Charters and the doctor, and now they dimmed and faded, shimmering an instant in the fading vision, and at last there was nothing but darkness, and in the darkness the ecstasy, and after the ecstasy, death and life.